ISN'T IT ROMANTIC

260 IMAGINATIVE WAYS TO EXPRESS YOUR LOVE

JOSEPH LIPARI

LEONARD JOBIN

Avery Publishing Group
Garden City Park, New York

Cover design: William Gonzalez and Rudy Shur
In-House Editors: Karen Hay, Marie Caratozzolo,
    Amy C. Tecklenburg, and Joanne Abrams
Typesetter: Bonnie Freid
Printer: Paragon Press, Honesdale, PA

Special thanks to the Diamond Information Center
for the use of the cover photograph.

For Heather,
        The Muse, moves through you!
                                L.J.

Printed in the United States of America

10 9 8 7 6 5 4 3 2 1

Contents

Acknowledgments

Special thanks to Heather, Melinda, Tony, Matt, and all our family and friends whose stories of romance have filtered down to us and made their way into our book.

We would also like to extend our thanks to the following people at Avery Publishing Group for their invaluable input into the making of this book: Karen Hay, Marie Caratozzolo, Amy C. Tecklenburg, Joanne Abrams, Elaine Will Sparber, Linda Comac, Elliot Glass, Evan Schwartz, Kerri Jenal, Shoshana Shur, Elizabeth Croteau, Nuno Faisca, Dina Goldstein, Eloise Caggiano, Lisa Cohen, and Harlan Krawitz.

Introduction

Welcome to the wonderful world of romance! Romance can literally improve the way you experience life. It may be something you're not very familiar with, but it is definitely not beyond your reach. All it takes is the right state of mind. If you train yourself to tune in to romance, you can develop the potential to make anything romantic.

So what is romance, anyway? Well, first let us establish early on that romantic behavior is very personal. No one can tell you that you're not romantic. That is something between you and your partner. So then, let's take a closer look at romance. Romance is not synonymous with love. Being in love does not necessarily imply romance. Ideally we use romance to express the love we feel for our mates. It is the way we communicate our love. This can be difficult, because love is such an abstract concept. Despite the overuse of the term, love, in essence, is something we carry within ourselves, and it is something that is very different for each of us. So how do we communicate this unique and abstract emotion to the person who inspires these feelings? We use romance.

Romance is the language that lays out the framework for our love. It expresses something that cannot accurately be revealed with our limited tools of language and gestures. We have to combine everything we know to get our point across. We must strive to be creative as never before and develop a strange new language of love; one filled with gestures and terms and examples that are unique to the individual romantic composition that every relationship possesses. There is an inherent sense of liberty in all of this because no rules exist. No one can put himself or herself in your place and know the variables in your life, so you must be the judge. You make the rules, and you are free to vary them as you see fit. Your romance is observed before a court of two: you and your lover.

Romance isn't a necessity in your life. You could well exist without it. However, romance is that little extra something that puts bounce in your step. It is the special topping on a pizza, the frosting on a cake. Ideally romance will develop into something much more than a little extra and become the highlight of your life. Romance is found in those sublime moments when all of the tedium and regulation of normal life fall away. At these times you are in the fortunate position of feeling love so deeply that all the other "junk" is forgotten. In fact, your love is so complete that you probably can't even tie down the conscious thoughts behind your romantic actions. Romance is like the expression of a language you have known from birth; it is second nature.

Romantic actions can be beyond the realm of your control. After you have spoken the language of a romantic gesture, you may find yourself amidst an indescribable sense of wonder that lingers preciously for you and your lover. You can be sure that your mate will appreciate your gesture and respect you—and the relationship itself—a little bit more. As an added benefit, the chances are good that your lover may reciprocate with a romantic gesture of his or her own. Romance also gives you a wonderful sense of doing something for someone else. True romance comes from the heart. You will find yourself saying and doing things that far outshine your normal level of passion and creativity. This is the true miracle. There is no question that we all have this special place within us and it takes only the right relationship and the proper mindset to draw it forth. If you are lucky enough to know this type of love, all we can say to you is count your blessings!

Because romance is not the same for every couple, this book is not intended to chart out a romantic schedule for you. That would fail hopelessly. Instead, we have provided a resource that can help inspire you in your pursuit of romance. There are a great many ways to apply romance to your daily life; correspondingly, we have described a large variety of romantic ideas for you.

Based on our culture in the late twentieth century, romantic occasions can be broken into two main categories: those that stem from a *responsibility* to act romantically, and those that are strictly *voluntary*. Occasions on which you would feel a responsibility for romance are relatively straightforward and include traditional days like Valentine's Day and Christmas, as well as personal landmarks like birthdays and anniversaries. This general category of required or obligatory romance is examined in Part I of this book.

Part II focuses on more spontaneous expressions of love. This section offers suggestions on how to create very special moments that heighten the importance of love between you and your mate, and goes on to show you how to turn even the most ordinary day into a romantic wonderland. To many, the more spontaneous actions presented in Part II are purer forms of romantic expression because they are unexpected. Both types, however, can be extremely effective. We will explore each of these basic kinds of romantic expression.

Part III of this book is a personal reference that will help you out with almost any romantic gesture. This allows you to keep track of important dates, preferences your partner has, clothing and jewelry sizes, sentimental information, and any new romantic ideas or variations of ideas. Fill in all of the relevant information about your relationship—and keep it updated—and use this when you are looking to add a special touch to your romantic ideas. Since any romantic action can benefit from a personalized touch, your personal reference may turn out to be the most frequently used part of this book.

Isn't That Romantic is filled with a wonderful sampling of heartfelt ideas that range from the basic, traditional to the highly unique. Everyone has read books or seen movies in which very traditional, old-fashioned romantic gestures—like giving roses on Valentine's Day—are expressed. We have included a number of these "old-fashioned" ideas throughout the book, generally injecting them with a creative twist.

Just about anything can inspire romantic ideas if you look at it with the proper frame of mind and then enliven it with your own signature touch. This book also touches on a number of funny and unexpected ideas. Romance can inspire life filled with both passion and fun.

In trying to create a romantic mindset it is crucial that you start by moving backwards, in the sense that you should strive to be a child again. Remember how as a child you reveled in play? One of the key ingredients for romance is the ability to be playful. Children are also incredibly creative. Feeling romantic encourages your creativity to flow. With playful and creative thoughts as your guide, you are bound to find romance.

Another focus of this book involves the presentation of special, spectacular, and unique ideas. As much as your expressions of love are of a personal nature, they may still benefit from a nudge in the right direction. As we compiled ideas for this book, we were consistently amazed at how the brainstorming of a single romantic idea inevitably led to numerous others. Our intention is to get your creative juices flowing by encouraging you with ideas, some simple, some elaborate. It is amazing what a little suggestion can do to help inspire you.

Finally, we present a number of ideas that involve the making of unique, one-of-a-kind gifts, things that carry that extra-special signature of love because they are products of your own two hands. (And it is often actions that speak louder than words.)

We also provide suggestions for commercial gifts that can be unique and special and sometimes customized to give them less of an off-the-shelf feeling. These types of gifts can be just as special as the homemade ones if they are presented the right way, maybe in conjunction with some of the ideas presented in this book.

Keep in mind not to overload your partner with all of your expressions of love at once. Subtle and quiet actions often make the point in a more effective fashion. Mix and match your romantic ideas to keep them fresh.

You also have to learn to judge both the moment and your partner when choosing your romantic strategies. Sometimes, a lighthearted, humorous approach is what's called for; at other times, a serious, straightforward expression of your love will be more appropriate. For example, your idea of romance may involve a bit of affectionate teasing, but if that makes your partner feel embarrassed or uncomfortable, obviously this is not a successful romantic strategy. Be sensitive to your mate's feelings, and observe which approaches elicit the best responses. Remember, the goal is express your love in a way that makes your partner *feel* loved.

It should also be mentioned here that we have been conscious of limitations when developing our romantic ideas. There are a number of entries in which the costs are minimal, but others that will require you to use practical judgement regarding your financial resources. But whether we are talking big bucks or small, your romantic expression is always going to come down to who you are, who your lover is, and the nature of your relationship. Combine these variables with an understanding of your resources, and you can develop a goal for your romantic intentions. And always keep in mind that romance should be fun.

In *Isn't That Romantic* we have provided you with the tools to help you build romantic moments, a vehicle that can be returned to again and again as you journey through life and draw forth the best of your romantic potential. These ideas should give you that little kick that gets you on a course for a personal expression of love in a language dedicated to you and your partner. Now, isn't that romantic?

Part I

Creating Memories for Special Days

 Think of a birthday party you may have had as a child. One where your friends came to your home dressed in their better-than-ordinary clothes, and you played games like Musical Chairs and Pin the Tail on the Donkey, before sitting down to a special dinner that ended with a candle-lit birthday cake, ice cream, and those great presents. Days like this were magical; ones that you will never forget.

I'm sure you would agree that we all grow up looking forward to special days. Remember how the whole world seemed to revolve around birthdays and holidays when you were young? You waited with such longing for these days that never seemed to come quickly enough. Feelings were further enhanced by a warm family setting and time spent with those you loved. When you got a little older and had a boyfriend or girlfriend, you added anniversaries and Valentine's Day to those days you considered special. With time, the birth of a child or other important events may have been added to your list. These are the special days that occur every year. The very reason they are special is because there are only a handful of them. If half of the days of the year were like birthdays, their specialness would decrease dramatically and their magic would disappear. There would be little cause for celebration.

For many, the very idea of romance conjures up the image of a special day. A day when one partner goes all out to make this day stand out in their lover's memory. A day when a person sets out to make the ordinary worries of the world vanish from their partner's shoulders. A day to become immersed in the innocence and freedom of childhood, and leave daily concerns behind. A time when everything is infused with wonder and your creative thoughts run freely. After all, isn't that the very way you feel when you're in love and look into your partner's eyes? A feeling that nothing beyond what you are seeing and experiencing could ever be more important?

Because most of us lead rather busy lives, it can be easy to forget about romance. We tend to get involved in the routine of our lives, and rely on the fact that there are set days throughout the year when romance takes the fore—when it is very much a responsibility.

This type of obligatory romance is often a person's main focus when he or she wants to express love to his or her partner. There are a number of days in a year that lend themselves very nicely to this idea of "special."

Birthdays, anniversaries, Valentine's Day, and Christmas are keenly associated in our society with gifts and romance. The aim on these days is to create the kind of "special day" we have just talked about. On the other side of the coin are the expectations that arrive with these special days. We have had it imprinted in our minds that such days require special treatment, and there is an inherent pressure that accompanies the arrival of a birthday or other holiday. As the number of days in a year for "special" plans can tend to get intimidating, it is hard for even the most creative of people to keep their offerings fresh and romantic. We can all use some help now and then. Planning something creative or romantic for birthdays, anniversaries, or other days that are inherently special can be a positive experience. And because they are set dates, you can design something carefully for them well in advance. Take advantage of the time and always be open to new ideas. Often, romantic inspirations spring up where you least expect them.

The planning and execution of your gift should be fun. It is very easy to become passionate about something and become immersed in its preparation. When you act out of love and caring for your partner, there is the potential for a special day for both parties. Dreaming up romantic ideas for your lover shouldn't become a worrisome task. With the help of this book, you can look forward to these special days as much as your partner does, just like you did when you first met. Go with the feeling and trust the results as you experiment with your expressions of love. Although all the entries found in Part I are located in specific chapters, there is no rule saying you can't customize them for a different occasion. Have fun and let those feelings of romance be your guide.

1. Birthdays

A birthday is the ultimate day for gift giving if you judge by greeting card stores. Walls and walls of cards are a constant reminder of the expectations that come with this day. If birthdays were not such a big production, there would be countless bankrupt businesses. You see, a birthday is very much a holiday that can be defined as an obligatory day of romance and gift giving. Society has led each of us to expect a form of exclusive attention on "our" day. This adds pressure as to how you should go about making your partner's special day live up to its reputation.

As a general rule, some of the finest birthday ideas can be obtained if you tune in carefully when your mate talks, and make mental notes of things he or she likes. Surprising your partner with one of these favorite pleasures is sure to delight. (It also lets your mate know what an attentive listener you are.)

Birthdays are extra-special romantic holidays because they call for one-way giving instead of two-way. This means you can truly display your love in its purest essence as your offering is focused entirely on your lover, with nothing expected in return. This is the very substance of romance. With this concentrated action you can have great fun and make your romantic gesture as elaborate or as streamlined as you like; you are in control and there are no rules except the fulfillment of your romantic goal.

ROMANTIC BIRTHDAY GIFTS

Often, simply buying a gift for your partner may not seem special enough—you may want to give something more unique, more personal. Here we have included some creative birthday gift ideas that range from from the very simple to the very elaborate. We have also suggested some extraordinary ways to present otherwise ordinary gifts. The following suggestions, should, at the very least, help you to start thinking romantically.

Certificates for Romance

Better than giving a store-bought gift, why not give your partner a variety of very thoughtful favors? Present that someone special with a book of one-of-a-kind gift certificates. Each certificate should contain a task for you to perform. The tasks can be anything—from the most mundane act to the most amorous. Your partner can then redeem the certificates at any time. Make each certificate unique by adding personal or humorous comments; and if you have an artistic flair, try designing them for an added personal touch. Creating the certificates on a computer would be ideal for duplication purposes. Here is a list of certificate suggestions:

❑ Give a back massage.

❑ Give a foot massage.

❑ Give a complete body massage.

❑ Give a back scratch.

❑ Act as your lover's servant for a day.

❑ Act as your lover's chauffeur for a day or week.

❑ Cook for your lover for a day.

❑ Wash and iron your partner's clothes (if not usually done by you).

❑ Vacuum the house (if not usually done by you).

❑ Cut the lawn (if not usually done by you).

❑ Do all of the household chores for a week.

❑ Do a specific household chore that your partner usually does and particularly dislikes.

❑ Wash your sweetheart's car.

❑ Prepare a candlelight dinner.

❑ Prepare a family dinner (if not usually done by you).

❑ Take the kids out so your spouse can relax at home.

❑ Take care of the kids at home so your spouse can go out.

❑ Serve your partner breakfast in bed.

❑ Do the grocery shopping (if not usually done by you).

❑ Brush your lover's hair.

❑ Give a sensuous scalp massage.

❑ Give a sensuous sponge bath.

❑ Give a blank coupon to be filled out by your lover.

In addition to offering your partner redeemable tasks, there are other things you can offer. For instance, maybe the two of you have different tastes in music and tend to "battle it out" over which radio station wins out while driving in the car. If this is the case, you can give your partner a certificate for exclusive car radio rights for one day (or one week, or one trip). Other redeemable gift certificate privileges or one-time wishes might allow your mate to:

❐ Have exclusive rights to the TV's remote control for the day.

❐ Choose the video for the evening.

❐ Choose the activity for a night out together.

❐ Decide where to go for a weekend trip.

❐ Choose where to go for a Sunday drive.

❐ Select the music to be played in the house for a day.

❐ Choose the television programs for the evening.

❐ Decide on the restaurant for the evening.

❐ Select a date to entertain friends.

❐ Go for an ice cream at any time.

❐ Choose a sexual activity.

You can make this gift even more interesting in the way you present the certificates. For instance, you can hand your partner a new certificate every hour or so throughout the day. Or you can put, say, ten certificates in a hat, then have your mate draw five of them for his or her birthday present. Another idea is to hide the coupons in different spots around the house or in the car, then let your mate play "finders keepers." Whatever your method, this madness is sure to make for a happy birthday.

The Wheel of Love

♥ This idea is a nice variation on the *Certificates for Romance* idea (page 12). The main difference is in the presentation. You will need two pieces of poster board and a pin or fastener. First, cut one piece of poster board into a large circle. Then, with a marker, divide the circle into as many pie-shaped sections as you have offers, and write one offer in each space. Next, place this circle in the center of the other piece of poster board. Secure the circle in the center with a pin or fastener that allows the circle to spin. At the top of the large piece of poster board, make an arrow, or perhaps a heart with its bottom point serving as an arrow. When your partner spins the wheel, the offer directly under the arrow is the one for you to fulfill.

Be creative and decorate your wheel of love with ribbons, colored poster board, or heart-shaped candies. You can also write a message on the back board, perhaps something like "I love you so much, I would _____ for you!" (Write this so that the blank is filled in by the offer that wins the spin.) Or you could simply write "I Love You" across the board.

In addition to being a fun game for both of you, this wheel is something you can save and use again and again. You can even collaborate to make new prizes to spin for. So let your lover spin the wheel, and let luck take over.

A Gift Collage

♥ Make a determined effort to show that you are interested in your lover's life. Create a collage of his or her favorite things. Include pictures of his or her pets, good friends, family members, schools attended, and just about anything else that reminds you of your lover. If a plain background is too bland for this project, use wrapping paper with a print that complements your chosen photos and clippings, or design your own background. You can also include items that will make your gift three-dimensional, such as a pressed flower, a meaningful party favor, or a matchbook from a favorite restaurant. A variation of this idea is to paint a picture that includes all of these "favorite" things. When your collage (or painting) is complete, have it framed to give it a professional look. This gift, which is composed of meaningful reminders to your lover, is sure to make a hit.

Garden of Love

♥ Create a gift made of plants and flowers to decorate your partner's home or office. Women especially find it very romantic to receive a gift of flowers. Why not really impress your mate with a portable garden that you have created your-self? First, select a unique decorative container and fill it with soil. Some good container choices include baskets, brandy snif-ters, china bowls, pieces of driftwood, and large shells. (If you are using a thick piece of driftwood for your planter, you must carve a hole in the wood to hold the soil.) Next, anchor a small plant or plants in the soil. Enhance the garden by adding things like pine cones, candles, rocks, or small statues. Decorate the container to make your gift even more unique.

Restoring Old Love

♥ One person's junk is another person's treasure. Most people have at least one "junk" item—an old lamp, a chair, a flower pot, a desk, a mirror, a bicycle—that has been sitting in the corner of their basement or a closet just waiting to be mended, reuphol-stered, refinished, or simply painted. A great gift idea here is to take that junk item and bring it back to life in whatever way necessary. You won't believe what a little creativity can do for something that otherwise would be considered useless.

A variation of this gift is to finish a project that your sweet-heart started but hasn't had time to complete. For example, sort loose photos into an album, or convert 8-millimeter home movies onto video cassettes. You partner will certainly feel gratitude for such a thoughtful gift.

A Gift From Home

♥ A gift that brings back fond memories is always a pleasant surprise. Purchase something unique from the town, city, or country where your lover grew up—preferably something that the place is well-known for. Every city or country is well-known for something, so it should not be too difficult to think of a gift. Or, if your partner has ever mentioned a special place from his or her childhood—a toy store, a sporting goods shop, a candy store—order a gift item from that place.

If your sweetheart grew up in a different city or town from the one you are living in now, try to get some photos of how that place looks now. Include pictures of the downtown area, the house in which your lover grew up, and schools he or she attended. Try to get photos of some of the special places and favorite hangouts that your partner has talked about. And don't forget about current pictures of childhood friends. Once your collection is complete, put the photos in an album and add captions if you like.

A simpler but less personal variation of this idea is to buy a current book about the city or town in which your partner grew up (if one is available). Present the book along with a promise to accompany your partner on a visit there in the near future.

Each of these variations can be a stirring reminder of one's roots. And a gift of this nature is a sure way to let your lover know how much you care.

"Frame That Action!"

Artists who create caricatures of people are a common sight at malls, arts and crafts shows, and on boardwalks and downtown streets. These amusing caricatures are usually of people involved in one of their favorite activities. If you have ever had one made, you probably got a kick out of seeing how the artist portrayed you. You can use this idea to create an exciting gift.

If your lover is actively involved in a sport, plays an instrument, is a fabulous cook, or has some other particular talent, take a photograph of him or her in action. Have the photo enlarged and professionally framed. Or take the "action" photo to an artist and have it stylized on canvas. Whether you choose a photograph or a painting, this gift is sure to make a lasting impression.

Handmade Love

Often the most precious and appreciated gifts are those that you make or create yourself. If you want to try your hand at making such a special gift, and you have lots of enthusiasm and some degree of talent, then give it a whirl.

If you're artistic, paint or draw something meaningful for your lover. If you're good at some kind of craft—needlepoint, decoupage, stained glass, woodworking, crewel, embroidery, origami—use your talent to create a unique gift. Perhaps you have the talent to write an original love song or a romantic poem. Or maybe you can knit or crochet an article of clothing for your mate.

If you would like to make something, but feel you either don't have the talent or don't have any good ideas, take a trip to your local library or bookstore. The shelves are always filled with books that are bursting with creative craft ideas. You can also find "how-to" books if you are interested in learning a specific craft.

Your extra effort in creating a gift yourself is invaluable in expressing your feelings of love. If possible, inscribe something on the gift as a constant reminder of your devotion.

Starry-Eyed Wishes

♥ How would you like to have a star named after you? Naming a star after your partner is a wonderful way of surprising him or her, and showing just how much you care. You can easily register a star in your lover's name through the International Star Registry. The presentation of this gift can be intimate and definitely romantic.

On a clear night, suggest a romantic walk in the moonlight. Point out some of the constellations, then casually point to the one that includes your partner's star. When your lover looks at you in confusion, hand over the registration papers, and explain that no star could shine as brightly as your love for him or her, but this was the closest you could come.

This is an original and thoughtful gift that shows how much your lover means to you. (For further information, contact the International Star Registry at 1–800–282–3333.)

Personalize Your Gift

♥ You can readily buy gift items such as coffee mugs and T-shirts that have captions and/or designs already printed on them. But why not buy your own item and decorate it yourself? Some items that are easy to decorate include solid-colored rubber rain boots, neckties, scarves, canvas shoes, T-shirts, mugs, sweatshirts, belts, and even umbrellas!

Most arts and crafts stores sell paints and markers specifically for use on different surfaces. Draw or paint a meaningful picture or design on the item and, if you like, add an "inside joke" (something personal between the two of you). And remember, you don't have to be an artist to do this; even if your gift has minor imperfections, the fact that you created the present yourself makes any little flaws or mistakes that much more special.

Distinctive Touches

♥ A drab-looking, poorly wrapped gift box can actually affect the impact of the gift it carries, regardless of how wonderful that gift is. Don't shortchange your gift by wrapping it carelessly.

After wrapping the gift neatly (in your own hand-designed paper, if you choose), you might want to add some finishing touches. For instance, you can further decorate the gift box with pictures, poems, or song lyrics. You can also use ribbon or lace to attach flowers, wrapped candy, or balloons to the box. To carry this gift-wrap idea a step further, use fresh flower petals or candy (preferably wrapped, and not made of chocolate) as filler for your gift box instead of tissue paper. See *Wrapping It All Up* (pages 96–97) for more gift-wrap ideas.

A Keepsake Gift Box

♥ Instead of the usual (or unusual) gift wrap for your present, why not make a gift out of the box itself? The simple method of decoupage is perfect for creating such a keepsake.

First, find a suitable box to house your gift. As your partner will be using the box long after he or she has removed the present, be sure to choose a box that is an adequate size and shape. Next, compile a collection of memorabilia, keeping in mind that it is best to use flat objects. Include such things as pictures (these can be photos as well as pictures cut from magazines), ticket stubs, playbills, postcards, greeting cards, and any other thing that holds special meaning for your lover. Arrange these articles on the outside of the box and glue them down. Once the glue has dried, cover the box with a coat of clear shellac. This will preserve the articles you have glued onto the box. When the shellac has dried thoroughly, it is a good idea to give the box another coat (and even a third coat if you like).

Now your gift can be presented to your lover in a very special gift box; one that will serve as a constant reminder of your love and caring.

Hide and Seek

♥ For fun, make your partner's gift-opening ritual memorable and exciting. Make it a little tricky and have your mate "work" a little for those presents. Here are a few ideas:

❒ If you're giving your partner a number of gifts for his or her birthday, create a treasure hunt. Hide the presents in different locations around the house. To start this game, provide your partner with a clue that leads to the location of one of the gifts. Along with this gift, leave another clue to the whereabouts of the next gift, and so on. At the last clue location, reward your partner with an extra-special gift (accompanied by a romantic kiss).

❒ Hide your partner's birthday present (or presents) in a spot inside or outside the house. To start this gift-finding adventure, tell your partner that you have hidden his or her present somewhere inside (or outside) the house. To help your lover, give clues as to whether he or she is on a "hot" or "cold" trail.

❒ Celebrate your partner's birthday with a Mexican theme, and hide his or her presents in a piñata. Using the traditional Mexican method, blindfold your partner and have him or her hit the piñata with a stick until it breaks. Of course, don't put any gifts inside the piñata that can be easily damaged.

Puzzle Clues

♥ When giving your partner a gift that can't be wrapped—a vacation, a club membership, tickets to an event—you can still be creative when presenting it:

❐ Buy a puzzle that doesn't have many pieces and assemble it. On the back of the puzzle, write the identity of your partner's gift. On the front of the puzzle, glue down a picture or an enlarged photo of something or someone meaningful to your loved one. When the glue has dried, follow the lines of the puzzle pieces to cut the picture into the proper shapes. Break the puzzle apart and put it back in the box. Your partner will have to put the puzzle together to discover the identity of the gift.

❐ In your partner's birthday card, write a short poem or note describing why you love him or her. Have the first letter of each line spell out the identity of your partner's gift. To help these initial letters stand out, you can either capitalize them, or write them in a color that is different from the color used in the rest of the poem. When you hand your partner the card, tell him or her that the identity of the present is somewhere in the card. Now you can sit back and enjoy watching your mate as he or she tries to figure out the hidden message.

❐ Write the identity of your partner's birthday present on a small strip of paper, and insert the paper into a fortune cookie. At the end of a special birthday dinner (of Chinese food, of course) watch the surprise on your loved one's face when he or she breaks open the fortune cookie and discovers a very special fortune. If you are in a restaurant, you can arrange to have the waiter bring the special fortune cookie to your table.

❐ Star in a special videotaped birthday message for your partner. You can make your message as humorous or serious or sensuous as you want. Somewhere within your performance, be sure to tell your mate the identity of your present. On your partner's birthday, pretend you have rented a movie. As you prepare to snuggle together in front of the TV to watch the movie, your mate will be shocked and heartwarmed when your "special" movie begins to play.

Birthday Cards

♥ A birthday wouldn't be complete without a birthday card. If you want to give that special someone a card that will be appreciated and remembered, create one of your own. You will have fun doing it and feel good about presenting it. Here are a few ideas for making your own birthday cards:

❒ Decorate the front of your card with a baby picture of your partner. You can include an amusing caption under the picture, or write something funny coming from the baby's mouth, maybe your partner's favorite saying or expression.

❒ Make a card using some of the different ideas presented in this chapter. For example, to decorate the card, use pictures of your partner's favorite things, as well as pictures of appropriate birthstones and/or flowers. If you have written a love song or poem for your partner, it can serve as the card's inside message. Of course, a simple sentiment from your heart can have just as much impact.

❒ Create a fun card by including such things as pop-up figures or cutout windows that open to uncover birthday messages.

❒ Construct a giant card in the shape of your sweetheart's age. On the card, write a list of things your partner has accomplished in his or her life, or a list of reasons why your partner should be happy.

❒ On the cover of your card, draw a cartoon-like character that represents your partner. Have the character in the middle of a favorite activity or deeply involved in a bad habit. Add some funny comments.

Other Distinctive Gifts

♥ If none of the gifts mentioned so far has tickled your fancy, you may want to check out the following list of gift possibilities:

☐ Imported craft items.

☐ Tickets for a cultural event.

☐ A music box.

☐ A movie poster.

☐ Silk bed sheets.

☐ A piece of jewelry.

☐ Handmade clothing.

☐ A piece of artwork.

☐ A kite (specialty stores often have unique varieties).

☐ A stained glass item.

☐ A candle and/or candleholder.

☐ A wall hanging.

☐ A picnic basket filled with favorite treats.

☐ Lingerie or silk boxer shorts.

☐ Fragrant sachets or netted packets of potpourri.

☐ A book of romantic poems.

☐ A new pet.

OTHER ROMANTIC BIRTHDAY IDEAS

In addition to giving your partner a gift on his or her birthday, there are plenty of other things you can do to make the day unique and special.

The Day That You Were Born

♥ This idea requires you to take a step back to the year your partner was born, and plan a thematic presentation around that year. Begin by dressing in the style that was the rage of the day. In the fifties, it was poodle skirts, rolled-up blue jeans, and saddle shoes; the sixties brought bell bottoms, fringed vests, love beads, and body paint; and the seventies saw the rise of platform shoes and leisure suits. Continue the theme by gathering as much memorabilia from that decade as possible. You can make a tape of some popular songs from that time and play the tape throughout the day. If your partner was a child of the fifties, you might choose to spend the evening in a fifties-style restaurant or club. You can either purchase or make a birthday present that incorporates this theme. Here are a few ideas:

❏ A poster of important events of the year or decade.

❏ A poster of clothing styles, cars, hair styles, and other things common to that time.

❏ A copy of a newspaper (or the front page of one) that was printed on your partner's actual birthday. This can be obtained through a library.

❏ A copy of a magazine that was issued near the time of your partner's birth.

❏ A poster of the Academy Award-winning movie of that year.

❏ A poster of statistics from the year your partner was born. Include such information as the cost of gas and other items; the number one song; the population of the country, state, city, or town; Academy Award winners; political leaders; famous headlines; and championship teams.

❏ A bottle of wine from the year of your partner's birth can signify that few things age quite as well as your partner.

A Traditional Favorite

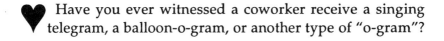 One of the longest standing birthday traditions in gift-giving history is that of giving flowers. How about a creative twist on this highly romantic gesture? For example:

❏ Plan a theme gift around your partner's favorite flower. Begin the day by serving her breakfast in bed. On the breakfast tray, have a bud vase with one or two of her favorite flowers. Later on, have her find a solitary flower in her car (or under the windshield wiper), and another bloom in her purse or briefcase. Arrange to meet for dinner at her favorite restaurant. When she arrives, greet her with a full bouquet of these flowers. As a final surprise, have her bedroom decorated with a liberal display of these blooms.

❏ Drape a bracelet, necklace, or other piece of jewelry over a fragrant bouquet of her favorite flowers.

❏ Tie up a bouquet of your partner's favorite flowers with a fancy ribbon. Attach a gift of jewelry to the ribbon.

A Birthday Melody

Romance and song have always gone hand in hand. An impassioned love song always seems to nudge a sentimental heart. Try to write and/or perform an original birthday song. If you are experiencing writer's block, try personalizing a song that already exists. If you want to take this idea one step further, record your love song. Some amusement parks, music studios, and music stores have recording booths specifically for such amateur recordings. This novel expression can be enjoyed and appreciated for years to come.

A Personal Messenger

Have you ever witnessed a coworker receive a singing telegram, a balloon-o-gram, or another type of "o-gram"?

This type of fun-filled idea can mean even more to your partner if *you* are the one who shows up in full costume to deliver the birthday cheer. Simply walk into your partner's workplace laden with helium balloons, cards, and gifts. While holding your lover's hands and looking into his or her eyes, sing "Happy Birthday." At the song's end, give your partner a big birthday kiss.

A Tribute to Life

One sure way to amuse your sweetheart is to put yourself on television. Make a video in which you play host to a *This is Your Life* television show. The "life" you toast (or roast, if your mate has a good sense of humor) is, of course, the birthday celebrity's.

In the video, interview your partner's friends and relatives; have them tell funny stories of your mate as a child or a teenager. Ask your partner's parents to relate baby stories of an appropriate nature. Film some snapshots of your lover as a baby, child, and teenager to fill in transitions between interviews. Find past grade school and high school teachers and ask them revealing questions about your partner's school habits and grades. Try to interview your partner's former bosses or coworkers (especially from funny or unusual part-time jobs your partner may have held during high school or college days). Move on to current stories about your mate as seen through the eyes of family and friends. If you have children, put them on film; ask them things about mommy or daddy. For the final interview, set up the video camera and film yourself. Give your own favorite anecdote about your partner and, of course, verbalize why you love this good sport. End the tape with family and friends singing "Happy Birthday."

A Fairy Tale Romance

If you don't mind putting a lot of time into a gift, consider videotaping your own short story in the form of a skit.

First, write a humorous or romantic tale about an event in your relationship (or borrow a plot from a well-known story, and substitute you and your partner as the main characters). With the help of some friends, film the skit, then end it with a special birthday wish for your partner. You can have great fun making the film, as well as watching it together.

You Didn't Think I'd Forgotten?

♥ Pretend to forget about your partner's birthday. Don't mention it for the entire day. As your partner arrives home from work, greet him or her with a beautifully wrapped present of a new outfit (perhaps a sport coat or dress). Pin a note to the outfit with instructions for your mate to change into it quickly— you have dinner reservations! Take your lover by the arm and set out for a fun-filled evening of romance.

The Power of Flour

♥ Very few purchased items can carry as much love as something made with your own hands. Since a birthday cake is a must, why not try baking it yourself? If you need a little help, check your local library, where you can find numerous books on cake baking and decorating. If you are the type who doesn't normally do much baking, be prepared to see your lover's eyes light up when he or she discovers that you made the birthday cake. Be sure to personalize the cake with a special message on top. You can also liven the cake presentation by putting a few sparklers amidst the candles.

Provocative Pictures

♥ Does a sexy picture of you seem like an unrealistic idea for your partner's birthday gift? Don't be so quick to dismiss this idea. A first-rate photographer can produce professional and classy pictures of this nature, and can actually make you feel comfortable during the shooting.

Flowers and Birthstones

Each month of the year is symbolized by a special flower and birthstone. You might choose a birthday gift for your lover with these symbols in mind.

Month	Flower	Birthstone
January	Carnation	Garnet
February	Violet	Amethyst
March	Jonquil	Aquamarine
April	Daisy	Diamond
May	Lily-of-the-Valley	Emerald
June	Rose	Pearl
July	Larkspur	Ruby
August	Gladiola	Peridot
September	Aster	Sapphire
October	Calendula	Opal
November	Chrysanthemum	Topaz
December	Narcissus	Zircon

The gift possibilities for your provocative pictures are endless. For example, you can simply slip the pictures into your partner's birthday card. Or, if you want to be a little more creative, surprise your lover by incorporating one of the pictures in his or her favorite part of the newspaper. (This will certainly break up the standard reading hour. And what are the odds that the paper will even get finished that night?) Other good hiding places for your photos include his or her car, briefcase, purse, cereal box, jacket pocket, and medicine cabinet. You can prepare a special photo album prepared with these pictures for a very personal gift.

Flower Power

♥ Get into the wild. Decorate your partner's car, inside and out, with wild flowers. For added effect, gather as many different types as possible. Tie a large ribbon around the vehicle and adorn it with a large birthday card. If you don't want to catch your partner completely off guard, warn him or her with a trail of flowers from the front door to the car. Record a birthday greeting on audio tape and have the tape ready and waiting in the tape deck. Your partner will be in for a drive to remember.

The Magic Hour

♥ Have you ever been awakened by a gentle tapping at your bedroom window in the middle of the night? To start your lover's birthday in grand fashion, at the stroke of midnight, show up outside his or her bedroom window to deliver a birthday card, a message, and a kiss. Flowers and balloons can further melt your lover's heart with romantic messages of love. If you are the theatrical type, this is a perfect moment to recite a love poem or sonnet. As you disappear into the night you can be sure that you will be leaving behind a warm heart.

Astrological Thought

Let the astrological mystic move through you. On your lover's birthday, consider giving a gift based on his or her astrological sign.

Month	Sign	Symbol
March 21–April 19	Aries	the ram
April 20–May 20	Taurus	the bull
May 21–June 21	Gemini	the twins
June 22–July 22	Cancer	the crab
July 23–August 22	Leo	the lion
August 23–September 22	Virgo	the virgin
September 23–October 23	Libra	the scales
October 24–November 21	Scorpio	the scorpion
November 22–December 21	Sagittarius	the archer
December 22–January 19	Capricorn	the seagoat
January 20–February 18	Aquarius	the water bearer
February 19–March 20	Pisces	the fish

Celebrate at Work

♥ Many people spend a great deal of time in the workplace. If your mate has a lot of friends at work, it might be nice to arrange a surprise birthday party for him or her at the end of the work day. Commence the activities by unexpectedly popping up with a candle-lit birthday cake. You and your partner's coworkers can then join in for a rousing rendition of "Happy Birthday." Bring snacks and drinks to make it a complete celebration.

If your partner's company isn't big on private parties, plan a surprise celebration at a bar or restaurant right after work. Have one of your mate's coworkers ask him or her to come out for a birthday drink. Your job, of course, will be to have the rest of your partner's colleagues at the party place ready and waiting to celebrate.

A Group Effort

♥ A very simple way to make your loved one feel extra special on his or her birthday is by making a large home-made card and having all of your mate's friends, colleagues, and family members sign it. The thoughtfulness and care that is shown by this effort can't help but set his or her heart soaring.

Another group effort idea to make your partner feel special is to persuade as many of his or her friends as possible to call to say happy birthday. Get friends from out of town, or those he or she hasn't spoken to in a while. Your sweetheart will love you (or hate you) for this one.

Housework Blues

♥ If your mate spends large portions of time doing dreaded housework, you can touch his or her heart by hiring a maid service for, say, once a week for a month. Then utilize you lover's free time to do some special things together. You can go on a romantic picnic, see a movie in the middle of the afternoon, or simply take a romantic walk together. Value this free time and keep the focus on romance.

An obvious alternative to hiring a cleaning service is to do your partner's tasks yourself without his or her knowledge. A break from cleaning the house or mowing the lawn is always welcomed.

A Surprise Breakfast

♥ You can always rely on the tried-and-true surprise of breakfast in bed to get your partner's birthday off to a romantic start. Try to sneak out of bed early to begin your morning surprise. Once you have prepared a special breakfast, add a few personal touches—a single flower in a bud vase will add a touch of class to the breakfast tray, and a birthday gift and card will certainly complement your thoughtful meal. Accompany the birthday breakfast with the morning paper and some music from your partner's favorite radio station.

The Fountain of Youth

♥ If your partner is feeling "old" and is not particularly excited about having another birthday, you can help him or her feel a little better by implementing the following scheme. Plan to take your partner out for a birthday dinner. When you call to make reservations, arrange for the waiter or waitress to ask your mate for the proper identification when he or she orders a glass of wine or a cocktail. (Use your judgement to decide whether your mate will find this flattering or annoying.) If done properly, even though your mate may know that he or she looks old enough to be served, the thought is sweet enough to put a youthful twinkle in his or her eyes.

A Happy Birthday Video

♥ Create a true "Happy Birthday" video for your partner. With camera in hand, proceed to film as many people as possible extending their happy birthday wishes to your part-

The Year of the Gift

In Chinese tradition, each year is represented by an animal. You might consider using the animal that symbolizes the year your partner was born for the theme of your present. A list of the animals that represent each year is presented below.

Animal	Year of Birth							
The Rat	1900	1912	1924	1936	1948	1960	1972	1984
The Buffalo	1901	1913	1925	1937	1949	1961	1973	1985
The Tiger	1902	1914	1926	1938	1950	1962	1974	1986
The Cat	1903	1915	1927	1939	1951	1963	1975	1987
The Dragon	1904	1916	1928	1940	1952	1964	1976	1988
The Snake	1905	1917	1929	1941	1953	1965	1977	1989
The Horse	1906	1918	1930	1942	1954	1966	1978	1990
The Goat	1907	1919	1931	1943	1955	1967	1979	1991
The Monkey	1908	1920	1932	1944	1956	1968	1980	1992
The Rooster	1909	1921	1933	1945	1957	1969	1981	1993
The Dog	1910	1922	1934	1946	1958	1970	1982	1994
The Pig	1911	1923	1935	1947	1959	1971	1983	1995

Along with using the appropriate animal as the theme for a birthday gift, you might also incorporate your mate's other personal themes—birthstone, flower, and astrological sign—into his or her present.

ner. Include people your partner knows well—family members, coworkers, friends—as well as those whose birthday greeting will surprise your mate. For instance, film your mail carrier, your neighbors, and even the UPS driver if you happen to get a delivery that day. Take your video camera to bars and restaurants that your partner frequents and film the staff members as they say (or sing) happy birthday to your mate. If your lover belongs to a health club, a bowling league, or another group or organization, walk in with your camera and film as many people you can find there (even those who may not know your partner) and have them extend their birthday wishes.

You can create a variation on this theme by adding a new set of birthday greetings to this film each year. Film some of the same well-wishers, as well as any new people in your partner's life.

This birthday video will take some effort, but the final product, which is sure to tickle your partner, will be well worth it.

A Special Trip

♥ If your partner has talked about a place that he or she has always dreamed of going, maybe now is the time for you to fulfill that dream. Send yourselves on a dream vacation. A "surprise getaway" is a classic gift that will draw you and your partner together.

Or, if possible, accompany your lover to a renowned event that he or she has always wanted to attend, such as:

☐ The World's Fair (if it is held that year).

☐ The annual Calgary Stampede in Alberta, Canada.

☐ Mardi Gras in New Orleans or Rio de Janeiro.

☐ New Year's Eve at Times Square in New York City.

☐ A space shuttle liftoff.

☐ The Cannes Film Festival.

☐ La Carnival in Quebec City, Canada.

❏   Winterlude in Ottawa, Canada.

❏   Oktoberfest in Munich, Germany.

If your lover is a big sports fan, arrangements to attend one of the following special sporting events would make a fabulous gift:

❏   The Olympics (if it is held that year).

❏   The Masters Golf Tournament.

❏   The Super Bowl.

❏   The U.S. Tennis Open.

❏   A Stanley Cup finals game.

❏   A figure skating championship.

❏   An NBA basketball finals game.

❏   The Indianapolis or Daytona 500.

❏   A World Series game.

❏   The European Grand Prix.

❏   The Tour de France.

❏   A World Cup soccer game.

❏   A championship boxing match.

A Long-Awaited Reunion

♥   Wouldn't it be wonderful to get together with one of your distant friends or relatives? This can be just as special for your partner. Reunions are always accorded memorable status. As a gift, arrange to have your partner meet an old friend or distant relative. For added excitement, make the reunion a surprise. Be sure to have a camera ready for this moment. A gift of friendship and family love beats a store-bought one any day.

Thematic Presents

♥ One birthday present is fine, but the more the merrier. Think of the excitement your partner will experience in receiving not one, not two, but many gifts. Make a collection of gifts with a specific theme in mind. For example, if your partner has a green thumb and enjoys working in a garden, you might give him or her a set of gardening tools, a pair of work gloves, a book on gardening tips, some flower seeds, a plant, and a special gardening hat. If your partner enjoys playing tennis, center his or her gifts around this sport. Include such things as private lessons; court time; a new tennis racquet, shoes, balls, and bag; and a tennis club membership.

Here are some more theme ideas and gift suggestions:

Theme	Gift Suggestions
Wine:	A bottle of wine, a corkscrew, a wine rack, a book on wines and winetasting, a set of wine glasses, shares of stock in a vineyard.
Beauty:	A bottle of perfume or cologne; a gift certificate for a professional manicure, pedicure, or facial; massage oils and bath oils; an assortment of specialty soaps, shampoos, and hand and body lotions; a bath sponge.
Coffee or Tea:	Specialty coffees and teas, a tea pot, a coffee pot, a cappuccino maker, a set of mugs or cups, a book on tea leaves or gourmet coffees.
Skiing:	New skiis, boots, or bindings; a pair of goggles and ski gloves; a new ski jacket, hat, or neck warmer; hand warmers; thermal underwear; lip balm; a ski vacation package.
The Office:	A name plate, a pair of bookends, a desk chair, a dictionary, a calendar, an office basketball hoop, some engraved pens.

Art:	Assorted brushes and paint types, an easel, some art books, a sketch pad, art lessons, a portfolio for his or her work.
Travel:	A money belt, some travel guides, a travel bag, translation books, a portable radio or cassette player with headphones, new luggage, a knapsack.

You may want to make a game out of presenting your collection of gifts. For instance, scatter the presents throughout the house and let your loved one go on a treasure hunt. Or give your partner one gift every hour or so, saving the most meaningful gift for last.

Leisure Activity Gifts

♥ Giving a gift that suits your partner's leisure-time interest shows a lot of understanding and consideration. Below is a list of leisure-type gifts that may fulfill one of these interests:

❐ Membership for a fitness club, CD club, book club, or video club.

❐ Tickets (season tickets, if affordable) to a sports event or a theater group production.

❐ A subscription to a favorite magazine.

❐ Lessons for such special-interest activities as acting, painting, calligraphy, craft making, dancing, golfing, karate, music, or tennis.

A Buried Treasure

♥ Hide your partner's birthday present (or presents) under a sea of balloons. Make sure you have enough balloons to cover the entire floor area, and make the pile as high as you want. Hide the gift (or gifts) somewhere beneath the pile. (To prevent your gift from getting stepped on accidentally, be sure to hide it in a corner or behind a piece of furniture.) This bit of birthday fun will make your partner feel like a kid again.

Final Romantic Thoughts on Birthdays

Romance can turn "just another birthday" into one that your partner will remember for years. Your partner's birthday comes around only once a year, which means that you have 364 days to come up with ways to pamper and please him or her. Giving a romantic birthday gift or celebration is an ideal way to shower your mate with affection. So go beyond the normal expectations on your partner's birthday and demonstrate just how special he or she is to you.

2. Engagements and Weddings

*T*he day you become engaged to be married and your wedding day are exceptional ones. There is probably nothing that receives as much thought as a plan for a distinctive proposal. As this moment generally happens only once in a lifetime, you should do everything you can to make it pleasantly ring with your personal touch, a moment you can proudly share with your children and grandchildren in the years ahead. There is almost nothing more romantic than telling another person you want to spend the rest of your life with him or her. As every detail of your proposal will be remembered and appreciated, it is important to think it through carefully.

Once the person you love has agreed to marry you, you can plan your wedding. Again, careful thought should go into this very special event. Whether you decide on a small private affair or a "Hollywood production," or whether you choose to get married in a church or while hanging from a cliff, your wedding day is one that deserves special attention.

IDEAS FOR ROMANTIC PROPOSALS

There are two basic styles for marriage proposals: the public announcement and the more private affair. Included here are some ideas for each type with an emphasis on presentation and originality. One general word of advice—don't try to improvise your proposal. Carefully plan your approach for a smooth delivery.

If you are leaning toward a public proposal, you may want to shout out your love in the middle of a mall, but with a little more thought, you can make your proposal one that will stand out from the standard shout. In this section we talk about a number of public ways to broadcast your proposal with the surprise factor amplified. However, you should be fairly certain of his or her answer or it could be more than a little embarrassing to have an audience witnessing your offer. Have fun with your plan, whatever it is, and enjoy the public display of your love. We also suggest that when you do employ a public proposal, follow it up later with a private celebration at home.

For the more common, private proposal, presentation and atmosphere are vital as you focus on a ritualistic gesture of love. And although we cannot tell you exactly what to say, we can advise you to keep your proposal honest, romantic, and full of love (write it down if you have to). We do, however, share some ideas on ways to ask for your loved one's hand.

Extra! Extra!

♥ Put your proposal in the form of a classified ad, and place it in the newspaper your partner usually reads. Phrase the proposal in such a way that your lover will know it is from you. Of course, your ad might be difficult to spot in the midst of all the other ads, so you will have to draw your sweetheart's eyes to it. With a colored pen or highlighter, circle the ad before your partner sits down to read the paper. When she turns to the classified section, your circled proposal will catch her eye.

This same idea can be utilized through other mediums.

Videotape your proposal and arrange to have it played during a late-night commercial break on a local television station. Or make an audio tape of your message and have a disc jockey broadcast it over the airwaves for you. Of course, if either of these ideas is going to be implemented, you must make sure your future fiancé is watching or listening.

Love on the Air

♥ If you would like to personally broadcast your marriage proposal over the radio, go for it. Talk to the program director at one of your local radio stations to make arrangements. It would be best to air your proposal during a late-night program that plays love songs. (If you can't get permission from a commercial radio station, you might have better luck with a college or university station.) Ask the disc jockey to play a special song that has meaning for you and your lover. At the end of the song, take over the microphone and deliver your message. (Be sure to have a written script in case you get nervous.) Of course, you have to somehow make sure your sweetheart is listening to the station during your proposal. She will surely be swept off her feet. Arrange to have a friend make a copy of the broadcast as a keepsake for you and your lover.

Sign Language

♥ Rent a billboard or a road sign that is on a route your partner frequents. You can either pay a company to professionally display your ad, or you can do it yourself. There are two things you should take into consideration when planning this type of proposal. First, make sure the sign is highly visible, not cluttered among other advertisements. Second, rent a sign or billboard in a low-traffic area, so when your partner notices the proposal, the surprise will not cause her to have an accident.

The Sky's the Limit

♥ Have you ever been on the beach or at an outdoor event and seen a small plane cross the sky while pulling a banner with an advertisement on it? Check your local yellow pages for a rental service of this kind and arrange to have your proposal stretched across the sky. A second and more complicated—and more expensive—airborne proposal is to have your offer spelled out with skywriting.

Boarding Passes

♥ Ask your partner to come with you to pick up a relative at the airport. Once there, have your proposal announced over the loudspeaker. The initial flood of embarrassment is sure to dissolve away to a blissful acquiescence when your sweetheart realizes exactly what is happening. After the acceptance, present tickets for a weekend trip to celebrate. Have the luggage already packed and in your car. In a matter of minutes, you are engaged to be married and off to celebrate for the weekend.

Sports Cohorts

♥ If you are both big fans of a local sports team, get tickets to see them in action. At some point during the game, arrange to have your proposal displayed on the scoreboard or announced over the public announcement system. The rest of the game will be memorable on two levels.

Now Showing . . .

♥ One way to publicly display your proposal is to show it in a movie theater. You might have a better chance of getting approval in a repertory or small theatre. After checking with the management for permission, find out the type of equipment used there, and have your proposal filmed on the apporporiate tape. Going to the movies will never be the same after this.

Say It With Song

♥ Revise the words to a well-known song so that it now includes your marriage proposal. Next, locate a bar or restaurant that has live entertainment—specifically, a singer. Meet with the singer and ask him or her to help you out with your proposal by singing your song. (The singer may even help you rework the song.) Imagine how surprised your lover will be.

A variation of this idea is to arrange to perform the song yourself. When your partner sees you head for the stage, she will probably be a little confused. But when she hears the special lyrics to your song, you are bound to knock her off her chair.

Marriage on the Menu

♥ A proposal in a restaurant can be done in several ways. There is nothing wrong with simply asking for your partner's hand in marriage over dessert and champagne, but we have two ideas here that are a little different. Both ideas require some preparation.

The first idea involves writing out your proposal on a sheet of stationery, then having the waiter slip it into one of the menus. (This should be arranged earlier in the day.) When you and your lover arrive at the restaurant, have a bottle of chilled champagne waiting for you at the table. While sipping the champagne, set the mood by telling your sweetheart how much she means to you and how much you love her. By the time the waiter brings the menus, feelings of romance should permeate the air. When your lover opens her menu, she will find your special note. Be sure to ask her what looks good on the menu. You can bring out the ring as a dinner special.

There is another way to pop the question that always surprises: Have the champagne poured and waiting before you are seated. When she gets to the bottom of the glass she will find the ring, and you must be prepared to propose. No cold feet allowed!

A Fairy Tale Proposal

♥ If your beloved is one who loves fairy tales and romantic gestures, this plan should blow her away. Here's your chance to be her knight in shining armor. However, you have to be able to ride a horse to carry off this proposal. To start, you must get out your telephone directory and find two things: a place that will rent you a horse, and a costume shop. Arrange to rent a horse for the afternoon (preferably a white one), then rent a knight's costume. Have your lover meet you at a park that afternoon in a specific spot. Now you can ride up to her, gallantly dismount, and bend down on one knee to propose. If she will let you, carry her away on horseback after she accepts your hand in marriage.

Déjà Vu

♥ A common but classy trick to employ for a marriage proposal is a re-enactment. The most obvious choice is to re-create your first date. Go to the same places and try to do the same things you did on that date. This time, however, add your profession of love and proposal of marriage to that good-night kiss.

A Floating Proposal

♥ Isolating yourselves from everyone else is a great way to set a romantic mood before popping the question. Rent a rowboat or a small motorboat and take her out on a peaceful lake. There is something timeless about the water that is a perfect accompaniment to the sentiments expressed in an offer of marriage.

Diamond Trivia

◆ Diamonds have come to represent the unbreakable bond of love between a woman and a man. They are used for engagement rings, wedding rings, and anniversary bands, and as tokens of love. But how did this symbolism come about?

◆ Diamonds were first discovered in India over 2,000 years ago. The word "diamond" comes from the Greek word "adamas," meaning unconquerable. Diamonds are the hardest known substance on earth, which is how they earned their name. There are many ancient myths about diamonds. In Greek mythology, diamonds were the tears of the gods; in Roman mythology, diamonds were splinters from the stars that Eros (the god of love) had made into tips for his arrows.

◆ In some cultures, before engagement rings became popular, a man and a woman might divide a piece of silver or gold in half when they became engaged. Each would keep a half to broadcast their engagement to be married. Eventually, this evolved into the custom of the engagement ring. It was the Italians who improved on this tradition by attaching a diamond to the ring to symbolize enduring love. The popularity of the diamond engagement ring grew rapidly after 1477, when Archduke Maximillian of Austria slipped one on the finger of his betrothed, Mary of Burgundy.

◆ Diamonds are not for engagement rings only; they are also used in wedding bands and many other types of jewelry. But whatever the reason a diamond is given, it has come to symbolize love.

Far and Away

♥ Plan your proposal to coincide with a time when you
and your lover are on a romantic vacation. At an oppor-
tune time during the trip, profess your love and present the
ring to your sweetheart. What makes this idea so appealing
is that you have the rest of the vacation to celebrate with fun
and romance.

Mystery Roses

♥ On the day you plan to propose to your lover, fill her day
with roses. Begin the morning by preparing her breakfast.
Have a single rose in a bud vase as a table centerpiece. Try to
place another rose in her briefcase or purse for her to discover
at some point during the morning. Then arrange to meet her at
a restaurant for lunch. When she gets to the table, have her find
another rose lying across her plate. While she is at work in the
afternoon, slip another rose on the front seat of her car or place
one under the windshield wiper for her to discover when she
leaves work. When she gets home and walks in the door, have
her find yet another rose along with a note instructing her to
meet you for dinner at her favorite restaurant. Finally, greet her
with a bouquet of roses as she walks into the restaurant. As she
takes the bouquet, gently place a tender kiss upon her lips. You
have set the perfect romantic background. Propose amidst this
atmosphere of flowers and love.

Detective Lessons

♥ An intriguing way to propose to your lover is by creating
a path of clues for her to follow that eventually leads to an
engagement ring. Begin by hiding the ring in a clever spot
somewhere in the house. As she walks through the door, pique
her interest by handing her a written clue that leads her to a
location where a second clue awaits. Have her solve two or
three more clues that eventually lead her to the ring and to your

heart, both hers forever. You might write out your proposal on a scroll, then roll it and fit it into the ring for her to find at the final clue location.

A Photo Proposal

♥ Use the idea of a photo album to make an engagement proposal. Create a photo album that documents the times and events you and your lover have shared. When you are ready to propose, make sure the two of you are alone and the setting is romantic. Bring out the album (this alone will be a pleasant surprise), and begin going through the photos together. If your lover is at all sentimental, going through this memorabilia will probably put her in a tender, emotional mood. On the last page of the album, have a photo of the two of you together. Under this picture, write out your proposal. If possible, fasten the ring to this page, as well. This beautiful album sums up your lives together thus far, and ends with the hope for a future together.

Greeting Card Love

♥ If you plan to propose on a day that is normally associated with the giving of a greeting card—Valentine's Day, Christmas, a birthday—you can spice up the Hallmark habit. Purchase a large greeting card. Write out your proposal on a smaller card, then slip it into the greeting card. When she opens the card, recite the proposal exactly as it is written. Offer her the ring in exchange for her heart. The idea of writing out your proposal is nice because you will always have a record of it; something you can go back to and reread as you move through your life together, something you can show your children and grandchildren.

A Surprise Engagement Party

♥ People often have engagement parties prior to their weddings. A union of two worthy souls is certainly deserving of such a celebration. However, we want to put a slight twist on that notion by having the party before the actual proposal. Arrange to have a group of your lover's friends and relatives waiting at a convenient party location. Get her boss or a family member to send her to the party place under the pretense of running an errand. Not only will your lover be stunned by the surprise of a party, she will be confused by it. Then it will be your turn to step forward and make it all clear for her as you ask her to spend the rest of her life with you. You can then celebrate your future together, along with the people who are near and dear to you.

The Secret Ring

♥ You may want to add the elements of fun and surprise to your private proposal. The most obvious way to do this is by presenting your beloved with an engagement ring in a clever fashion. Use your imagination and come up with a unique idea. Listed here are a few suggestions:

❏ If your partner has a pet dog or cat, attach the engagement ring to the animal's collar. After you have proposed, call the pet into the room to deliver the all-important jewel.

❏ Put the engagement ring on a necklace, then place the necklace around a stuffed animal. You can buy a new stuffed animal or use one of her personal favorites for this idea.

❏ Put the engagement ring inside a balloon. Inflate the balloon (don't use helium) and write "Will You Marry Me?" across the front. Include this "special" balloon in a bouquet of multi-colored helium-filled balloons. (Again, for obvious reasons, make sure the balloon that holds the ring is not filled with helium. As an added preventive measure, tie the string of the ring-filled balloon to your wrist. In case the balloon bouquet gets loose, this will keep the special balloon from being carried up and away with the others.) When your lover opens the door, step inside and present her with the bouquet. It shouldn't take long for her to notice the balloon with your proposal.

Here's another way to surprise your lover with a ring-filled balloon. First, empty the contents of a closet in your sweetheart's home. Next, tie a string to the special balloon and suspend it from the closet ceiling (eye-level is best). The next step is to fill the entire closet with loose inflated balloons. When your lover opens the closet door, she will find herself in the midst of a balloon waterfall. After the initial shock, she will notice the special balloon that is still hanging in the closet.

Another idea for the ring-filled balloon is to place it in a room that is filled waist-high with other balloons. After telling her that one of the balloons is special, watch her enjoy herself as she wades through this sea of balloons, trying to find the distinctively important one.

❐ It is common for marriage proposals to coincide with holidays or other special days; this enhances the already-festive atmosphere. If you plan to propose at Easter, you can hide the ring inside a plastic Easter egg. At Christmas, you might wrap the ring in an oversized gift box to throw her off. To add a bit of drama to the unwrapping, you can place the ring box inside a slightly larger box, place that inside yet another box, and so on. All the boxes should be gift-wrapped so that your intended will have to unwrap a series of boxes before she gets to the ring. Or place the ring in the bottom of a Christmas stocking. If you plan to propose to your lover on her birthday, write your proposal in frosting on top of the birthday cake or include a written proposal in her birthday card.

❐ If you plan on proposing to your lover over a candle-lit dinner that you have prepared yourself, try the following surprise tactic. Hide the engagement ring by freezing it in an ice cube. Use that cube in her drink that night.

❐ Write your proposal on a small piece of paper. Insert both this paper and the engagement ring (if possible) in a fortune cookie. Hopefully, when she breaks open the cookie, her fortune will agree with her.

❐ Place the ring in an ordinary spot—her purse, for instance.

Then ask her to get something from her purse. When she looks inside, she will discover your big surprise.

IDEAS FOR ROMANTIC WEDDINGS

It doesn't matter if your wedding is large or small, you can always add personal intimate touches to create a romantic atmosphere on that day. (Small affairs are often more conducive to creating romantic moods.) Attempt to have the ceremony and reception reflect your personalities. Focus on where the wedding is to be held and how it is arranged. This section includes some ideas to help you plan for a romantic wedding.

There's No Place Like Home

♥ Home can be a beautiful place to have a wedding (have you seen the movie *Father of the Bride*?) If your house or yard is spacious enough, this homey environment can be a wonderful place to exchange your marriage vows. Many catering services offer extensive buffet-style menus for just such events, as well as people to help set up and serve the food. They also provide clean-up help when the party is over. If you want the reception held outdoors, you can rent a large tent to accommodate your guests. These rental companies also supply tables and chairs, which they set up however you wish.

A wedding at home can be a bit of work, but it can also be great fun. Best of all, you will be celebrating in a comfortable place that you know and love so well.

A Garden Festival

♥ If you want that at-home feeling, but can't stage your wedding at home, consider holding the ceremony in a botanical garden. There are many establishments that offer such services. The natural setting of a botanical garden is perfect for a small wedding.

A Princess Bride

♥ If you and your fiancé are unconventional types, a medieval-style wedding may be just right for you. Throughout the United States there are Renaissance restaurants that offer medieval-theme dinners. Some of these places also cater weddings.

For a medieval-style wedding, the groom dresses as a knight, while the bride dresses as a princess. Your medieval-style wedding feast should include a lavish spread of hand-held foods (no utensils allowed) such as roasted chickens, racks of ribs, corn on the cob, and round loaves of bread. Many Renaissance restaurants also offer entertainment, which may include juggling and acrobatics performed by "court jesters," musical interludes offered by "wandering minstrels," and lyrical poetry recited by courtly "troubadours." Some places have outdoor courtyards where "jousting" events are held.

This out-of-the ordinary wedding event can be great fun. Just be sure to indicate on the invitations the type of wedding your guests should expect, and encourage them to come in proper medieval attire.

Love Boat Wedding

♥ Do you and your partner enjoy the water and simply love boats? Some cruise ships and steamboats offer banquet facilities for private parties. Check them out. Such a romantic setting can make your wedding and reception a voyage to remember.

Beach Blanket Wedding

♥ Another novel place to have a wedding is at the beach. Everyone knows the beach is a great place to catch some rays and toss around a frisbee, but it can also substitute as a great party location. If you choose this site for your wedding, you can have a lot of fun with it. For instance, you can have the bridal party wear matching "wedding" bathing suits. At the beach reception, include a barbecue, some swimming and surfing races, a beach volleyball game (bride's side versus groom's side), and a late-night bonfire with marshmallow roasting and a singalong.

Wacky and Wild

♥ If you and your partner are wacky and wild, you may choose to take your wedding vows in an equally wacky location. For example, if you both like mountain climbing, hold your ceremony on top of a mountain. Of course, you will have to limit the number of guests you can have in attendance; however, this should not stop you from having a bigger reception afterwards. Here are a few more unconventional locations to hold a wedding ceremony:

❑ On horseback.

❑ On a roller coaster.

❑ At a circus.

❑ On a merry-go-round.

❑ In an airplane.

❑ While skydiving.

❑ While bungee jumping.

❑ While scuba diving.

❑ On a baseball diamond.

❑ On a ski slope.

❑ On the eighteenth hole.

❑ While hang-gliding.

❑ While parasailing.

A Grand Event

♥ A wedding is truly a grand event. Keeping the "grand" idea as a theme, hold your wedding in conjunction with

The Story of the Wedding Ring

Ô Wedding rings are a tradition that dates back to ancient times. As far as we know, primitive men and women did not have wedding ceremonies like we do today, but early grooms are believed to have had an interesting way of showing their intentions. A man would weave a special cord and tie it around the waist of the mate he wanted. The belief was that when he did this, her spirit entered his body and she was bound to him eternally.

Ô The ancient Egyptians were the first people known to take their symbol for eternity, the circle, and use it to signify the marriage union. They placed a ring on the third finger of the left hand (a tradition we still have today) because they believed that the "vein of love" ran directly from this finger to the heart. These ancient rings were made of everything from leather to bone to metal.

Ô Gold wedding bands—probably the most popular type of wedding ring in the world today—were once a sign of great prosperity. Wedding rings were also once used as part of a groom's bride payment in arranged marriages, and showed the groom's noble intentions. In the medieval and Renaissance periods, royalty and the wealthy often gave wedding rings encrusted with different gems. The plain wedding band supposedly became popular when Queen Mary I of England married King Philip II of Spain in 1554. She insisted on a simple ring without any gems.

another grand event or place, such as Times Square on New Year's Eve, or Super Bowl during half time. A major local event such as a winter carnival or a jazz festival is another possible place to hold an extra-special wedding ceremony.

Island Paradise

♥ Instead of arranging a traditional wedding, you may plan a romantic getaway and get married on some sun-drenched tropical-island paradise. You can hold your ceremony in a unique and exciting setting, and you won't have to go far for the honeymoon! Invite only a best man and a maid of honor, or do it all by yourselves. After the ceremony, call home to announce the big news. When you return home, plan a wedding reception with friends and family.

A Striking Entrance

♥ In addition to the actual type and location of your wedding, you can stamp your personal signature on this event from the start with a memorable entrance. A refined and classy entrance can be achieved by arriving at the ceremony or reception in a horse-drawn carriage or an antique car. Or go a little more flashy by pulling up in a Ferrari convertible. How about an elegant entrance in a Rolls Royce? Another nice entry, if the wedding happens to be held near the water, is by boat. If you are the type who likes to shock, think of the entrance you will make by pulling up on a motorcycle! No matter how you do it, your entrance is sure to establish a tone for the wedding that follows.

The Romantic Getaway

♥ Want a really sensational, romantic finale to your wedding day? At the end of your reception, arrange a romantic getaway in a hot air balloon. After boarding the balloon, wave goodbye to your guests as you float toward the heavens. Have

The First Honeymoon

 The origin of the term "honeymoon" is something of a mystery, but according to folklore, it stems from marriage practices of days long before wedding ceremonies ever existed. Instead of having a public marriage rite, a man would very often simply abduct his chosen bride, and would go into hiding with her for a period of time, until her (possibly enraged) relatives stopped looking for them. While in hiding the newlywed couple would supposedly drink a special type of wine made from honey. The period of hiding traditionally lasted for a month, enough time for the moon to go through all its phases; hence, the name honeymoon. Today, many couples still keep their honeymoon plans a secret.

champagne and flowers on board, and throw the bridal bouquet to the waiting maidens as you take off.

Sing Your Heart Out

♥ Let everyone know how much you love your new spouse. If you have the talent, sing a love song to your partner during the wedding reception. This is a wonderful romantic gesture that your partner will always remember. (Try to have this captured on videotape.) It will be the highlight of your wedding day.

ROMANTIC WEDDING GIFTS

A special wedding gift for your partner is a symbolic gesture that is representative of your eternal love. Any one of the following suggestions may be just right for you.

The Gift of Love

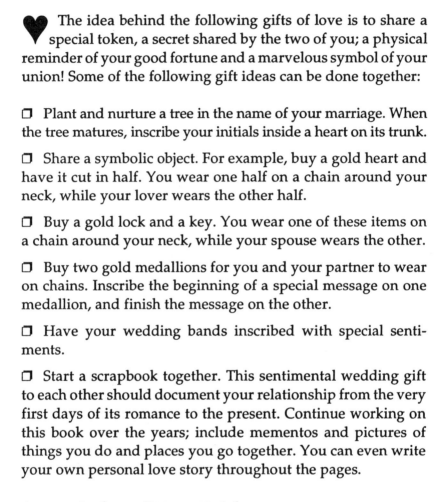 The idea behind the following gifts of love is to share a special token, a secret shared by the two of you; a physical reminder of your good fortune and a marvelous symbol of your union! Some of the following gift ideas can be done together:

❑ Plant and nurture a tree in the name of your marriage. When the tree matures, inscribe your initials inside a heart on its trunk.

❑ Share a symbolic object. For example, buy a gold heart and have it cut in half. You wear one half on a chain around your neck, while your lover wears the other half.

❑ Buy a gold lock and a key. You wear one of these items on a chain around your neck, while your spouse wears the other.

❑ Buy two gold medallions for you and your partner to wear on chains. Inscribe the beginning of a special message on one medallion, and finish the message on the other.

❑ Have your wedding bands inscribed with special sentiments.

❑ Start a scrapbook together. This sentimental wedding gift to each other should document your relationship from the very first days of its romance to the present. Continue working on this book over the years; include mementos and pictures of things you do and places you go together. You can even write your own personal love story throughout the pages.

A Reminder of Your Faith

After you have been married a number of years, think about how nice it would be to remember the very thoughts and feelings you both experienced when you were newlyweds. Shortly after you are married, as a special wedding gift to each other, write down all the reasons you love your new spouse. Be sure to include all of the feelings and emotions you experienced on your wedding day. Store this "testimonial" in a safe place and periodically read it together (anniversaries are the perfect time). It is a wonderful reminder of the special reasons you married your partner.

On This Special Day

♥ Many newly married couples save tokens and mementos from their wedding day to keep along with their wedding album. If this idea appeals to you, take it a step further and collect other memorabilia that reflect things that were happening in the world on or around your wedding day. For example, keep a copy of the day's local newspaper; make a videotape of some of the popular television shows that aired during the week you were married; obtain current magazines on fashion, cars, movie stars, sports, music, and news. To these items, add a list of the top songs, books, recording artists, and movies of the day. Store this collection in a special place as part of your wedding memorabilia.

Final Romantic Thoughts on Engagements and Weddings

The moment when you propose to your love is likely to be one of the most memorable of your lives. Since you have no doubt put a lot of thought into asking your mate to marry you, you should put a little extra time and effort into making this moment special. You want your spouse to look back on this moment with fond thoughts.

Your wedding day is equally deserving of romantic forethought. Delve into your partner's deepest expectations of this special day and try to make his or her dreams come true. Whether you choose a large ceremony or a small one, take this opportunity to show your new spouse—and the world—how you feel about him or her. Your wedding day is a day focused on your love for each other, and your commitment to spend your lives together. What a wonderful way to set the tone for a romantic life together.

3. Anniversaries

M ost married couples will tell you that their wedding day was one of the the most precious days of their lives. Marriage is a solemn and reverent event in our culture. To be happily married is no simple task, and if you have achieved this, then you and your spouse should be honored. An anniversary is the day to remember the reasons you fell in love with and married your mate, and why you are looking forward to the future together. It is also a wonderful day to plan something special. Put your heads together and honor this day that is different from all others because of the unique meaning it holds for you.

ROMANTIC ANNIVERSARY GIFTS

It is lovely to exchange cards and gifts of flowers, candy, and jewelry on your anniversary. However, you might also appreciate giving, as well as receiving, a more unique gift for this romantic celebration.

Romantic Trivia Game

♥ Together with your spouse, make up a romantic trivia game in honor of your anniversary. On index cards, each of you privately write down as many trivia questions about yourselves and your relationship as you can think of. When both of you have a substantial number of questions, begin the game. Take turns asking each other questions. (The idea here is to have fun, so don't get upset if your spouse doesn't know some of the answers to your questions.) It is up to the two of you to make the rules. For example, you might decide to offer points for correct answers. The spouse with the most points at the end of the game (or round) wins a prize—perhaps a sensuous back massage, a coupon for breakfast in bed, or full rights to the TV remote control for a day. No matter what the rules or the prizes, you are bound to enjoy this game together. Here are some suggested trivia questions:

❑ Where did we go on our first date?

❑ What was the first movie we saw together?

❑ In which restaurant did we first have dinner together?

❑ What was my phone number when we first started dating?

❑ What car was I driving when we met?

❑ What happened when you met my parents for the first time?

❑ What was my address when we first met?

❑ Where did we first kiss?

❑ Where did we first make love?

❑ What is my favorite movie, color, book, food, animal, TV show, song, candy, or flower?

❑ Who is my favorite actor, athlete, hero, comedian, teacher, or singer?

❑ Where was my favorite vacation spot, restaurant, city, country, or campsite?

❏ What was the first gift I ever gave you?

❏ What was the first gift you ever gave me?

❏ What were you wearing the first time we met?

❏ What was I wearing the first time we met?

❏ What was the song we first danced to? Where were we?

❏ What is "our" special song? (If your spouse answers this question correctly, have the song ready to play, and ask for a dance.)

❏ What was your favorite perfume/cologne when we first started dating?

Also include questions specific to your jobs, personal preferences, friends, and experiences. You can even raise the stakes by calling for the removal of an item of clothing for each wrong answer.

This game may seem like a lot of work, but it has a high probability for success. Keep the trivia cards and play the game every few anniversaries with the addition of new questions.

The Anniversary Wheel

♥ This game is a nice variation on the *Certificates for Romance* gift idea (page 12). The difference is in the presentation. You will need two pieces of poster board and a pin or fastener. First, cut one of the pieces into a large circle. Then, with a marker, divide the circle into a number of pie-shaped wedges. Write one gift offer in each wedge. Next, place this circle over the remaining piece of poster board. Secure the circle in the center with a pin or fastener that allows it to spin. Draw an arrow at the top, or perhaps a heart with its bottom point being the arrow. Have your spouse spin the wheel. The offer directly under the arrow is the one you are required to fulfill.

Be creative and decorate your wheel of love with ribbons, colored paper, or heart-shaped candies. You can also write a message on the back board, perhaps something like, "I love you so much, I would ____ for you!" (The blank should be filled in by the offer that wins the spin.) Or you could simply write, "I Love You" across the back board.

In addition to being a fun game for you both, this wheel is something you can save and use again and again. You can even collaborate on new prizes to spin for. So let your lover spin the wheel and let love take over.

Anniversary Crossword

♥ For your first anniversary, create a crossword puzzle that includes all of the significant things that occurred during your past year together. Make up clues that are specific to things you did, funny moments you shared, people you met, places you went, and any other things of this nature. You can create a new puzzle for each anniversary or build off the old puzzle. (Although it isn't necessary, be aware that there are computer software programs available for making crossword puzzles.) One thing is certain, you'll find your spouse looking forward to this annual trip through your lives.

Cover Story

♥ More than likely, you and your partner are not world famous, so your picture on a popular publication can carry a powerful shock. Select one of your favorite magazines and put a picture of the two of you on the cover (many novelty shops do this type of thing). Write some articles and a few advertisements that illustrate your relationship, and paste them within the magazine along with an appropriate picture or two. Write ads that cater to your spouse's passions; replace existing articles with your own humorous accounts of such things as your mate's quirks or personality traits, projects you

Anniversary Traditions

Traditionally, each anniversary is associated with a specific material. Following this tradition means selecting an anniversary gift made of that particular material. In more recent years, an alternate list of gift suggestions has been affiliated with each anniversary year. Both lists are presented below.

Anniversary Year	Traditional Gift Material	Modern Gift Suggestion
1st	Paper	Clocks
2nd	Cotton	China
3rd	Leather	Crystal/Glass
4th	Linen/Silk	Electrical appliances
5th	Wood	Silverware
6th	Iron	Wood
7th	Copper/Wool	Desk sets/Pen and pencil sets
8th	Bronze	Linens/Laces
9th	Pottery/China	Leather
10th	Tin/Aluminum	Diamond jewelry
15th	Crystal	Watches
20th	China	Platinum
25th	Silver	Sterling Silver
30th	Pearls	Diamonds
35th	Coral	Jade
40th	Ruby	Ruby
45th	Sapphire	Sapphire
50th	Gold	Gold
55th	Emerald	Emerald
60th	Diamond	Diamond
75th	Diamond	Diamond

have accomplished together, and maybe an embarrassing story or two. If you have kids, be sure to mention them in the magazine. You might also choose to touch on some deeply intimate and moving memories the two of you might have shared. A lot of work, perhaps, but this self-contained master-piece is a real treasure.

Gifts From the Past

♥ An anniversary is a time to honor your wedding day. It is also a time to relive the feelings you experienced on that special day. Be sure that you have preserved some of these unique reminders. For instance, have your wedding vows printed on parchment or other fancy paper, then have them framed. You can recite these vows to each other again. Have one of your wedding invitations framed as well. On your anniversay, sit down together and look over these special items along with other mementos of your wedding day, such as your guest list, a picture of the bridal party, a copy of your "wedding song," and your wedding album. Warm feelings of love and romance are sure to flood your hearts during this time of reminiscing.

Lover's List

♥ Explore your own utterly distinct love for the one and only love of your life. Make a list of some or all of the following:

❑ The praiseworthy (and also the more subtle, yet moving) things your lover has done for you.

❑ How your lover's thoughtful gestures make you feel.

❑ The reasons your lover is important to you.

❑ The reasons you married and love your partner.

❑ The feelings you had when you first met and fell in love with your mate.

Once you have compiled your list, decide on a special way to present it to your spouse. You can, for example, write out your list on a fancy scroll. Roll up the scroll, tie it with a ribbon, and present it to your spouse on your anniversary. Or you can write your list on parchment and have it framed. You might have the list written in calligraphy. (Either hire a service to do this or do it yourself if you know how.) One final idea for presenting your spouse's praiseworthy traits is to print them out on individual cards, then hide the cards around the house. Your spouse will be thrilled with the discovery of each card.

Photo Fun

Create an anniversary gift with photographs. One idea is to make a witty story about your loved one and put it in a comic strip format. Write out captions on white paper, then paste them on the photos. Another idea for a photo gift is to create a collage of favorite photographs. Once you have mounted the pictures, have the collage laminated or framed. These types of gifts are fun to create and make great keepsakes.

Scrapbook

Make a scrapbook of special romantic memories. You can include:

❑ Anniversary, Valentine's Day, and birthday cards.

❑ Cards that came with flowers.

❑ Golf/bowling scores.

❑ Love letters.

❑ Locks of hair.

❑ Newspaper clippings.

❑ Photographs.

❑ Poems.

❑ Postcards.

❑ "Remember when" notes.

❑ Restaurant mementos.

❑ Ribbons from special gifts.

❑ Theater programs.

❑ Ticket stubs.

❑ Vacation souvenirs.

❑ Wedding invitations.

❑ Wine labels.

❑ Pressed flowers.

Include any other memento that recalls romantic times. Bring out the scrapbook every year to reminisce over and to update.

Special Balloons

♥ How about carrying a simple anniversary balloon greeting to a more personal level? Purchase some plain balloons and embellish them with your own messages. You might use some items from the *Lover's List* gift idea (page 64). Be sure to fill the balloons with helium; nothing else will substitute. Tie each balloon with long ribbons. For an added touch, tie small gifts to some of the ribbons—a small bottle of perfume or cologne, tickets to a play or sports event, or maybe a dinner invitation.

A Special Portrait

♥ Most couples have at least one photograph of themselves in a loving pose. What they rarely have is a painting of themselves. For an exquisite gift, have a portrait of yourselves professionally painted. You can either pose for the artist, or give him or her a photograph to use as a model. This gift will be enjoyed by you and by future generations.

Symbols of Love

♥ An anniversary is a time for reflections of your wedding day and of the vows you took. Reaffirm your love with a symbolic gift. Here are some ideas:

❑ A bottle of wine from the year of your marriage.

❑ A piece of jewelry to which you can add something each year, like a pearl necklace or a charm bracelet.

❑ Anniversary bands that are inscribed with special messages of love.

❑ A tree or shrub to plant each year in commemoration of your anniversary.

A Video Depiction

♥ *A Fairy Tale Romance* (page 26) proposed the idea of creating a short film about your lover or your lives together as a birthday present. This same idea can be customized for your anniversary. For the anniversary version, the story line can focus on a comic portrayal of your first date, your spouse's first meeting of your parents, recollections of your wedding day, and any other significant romantic episodes from your past. You can include a glimpse into the future and portray what you think your married life will be like in ten or fifteen years. Be sure to end your film with a fervent expression of your love and a wish for a wonderful anniversary.

A Video Tribute

♥ Here is another video gift idea of a personal and romantic nature. Make the film a documentary about your lover. Interview your spouse's friends and family members. Have them tell an interesting story or two about your spouse. Interview your kids and ask them why they love mommy or daddy. Finally, put yourself in front of the camera and relate some of your own warm stories about your lover, and the reasons why he or she means the world to you. This lasting testament is a powerful statement of your love.

Anniversary Cards

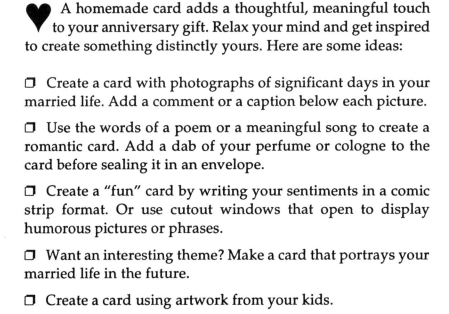 A homemade card adds a thoughtful, meaningful touch to your anniversary gift. Relax your mind and get inspired to create something distinctly yours. Here are some ideas:

❒ Create a card with photographs of significant days in your married life. Add a comment or a caption below each picture.

❒ Use the words of a poem or a meaningful song to create a romantic card. Add a dab of your perfume or cologne to the card before sealing it in an envelope.

❒ Create a "fun" card by writing your sentiments in a comic strip format. Or use cutout windows that open to display humorous pictures or phrases.

❒ Want an interesting theme? Make a card that portrays your married life in the future.

❒ Create a card using artwork from your kids.

Whether your card is humorous or serious, be sure to include a romantic reflection of your years together.

OTHER ROMANTIC ANNIVERSARY IDEAS

Your anniversary is a day that deserves a special, romantic celebration. Try one or more of the ideas in this section to make the occasion especially memorable.

Honeymoon Revisited

If possible, as a special anniversary gift to yourselves, go back to the place where you spent your honeymoon and try to re-create the magic. If you are not able to return to your honeymoon site, on your anniversary, decorate your home to create the mood of that special place. For instance, if you honeymooned in Hawaii, try to give your home that "island paradise" feel. Drape leis around the room and around your necks, wear brightly colored floral shirts (or maybe a grass skirt), put on some Don Ho music, and celebrate with creamy piña coladas and juicy pineapple spears. Use your imagination and enjoy, but remember, one of the key ingredients to a successful honeymoon is a minimum of distractions. So take the phone off the hook, unplug the television, and do not answer the door. Make it a time for the two of you only.

Laying a Trail of Love

♥ On your anniversary, lay out a mysterious path for your spouse to follow. Start with a trail of flowers or rose petals along the sidewalk or up the driveway. Have the trail lead to the front door, which should be decorated with festive streamers and a "Happy Anniversary" banner. Tack a note on the front door instructing your spouse to follow the flower trail. Inside the house, have the path lead your spouse to the stereo, where you will be waiting. Put on a slow, meaningful love song and ask your spouse for a dance. When the dance is over, take your lover by the hand and continue to follow the path to a beautifully set dining room table. After a sumptuous dinner, continue following the path from the dining room to a warm, sensuous candlelight bath. Finally, end the trail in the bedroom, which should be bathed in candlelight. Have the bed covered in satin sheets, and have a bottle of champagne on ice waiting next to the bed.

Limousine Romance

♥ To celebrate your anniversary, take a short vacation in your own city. Arrange to have a limousine take you to an elegant restaurant where you have dinner reservations. After dinner, continue with a tour of the city while having your own private party in the back of the limousine. Eventually, have the limousine present you at the door of a four-star hotel (maybe one you have never been to before) where you can spend the night together.

The undisputed freshness of this adventure in your own hometown is sure to make for a wonderful anniversary celebration.

Love for All Time

♥ The concept of true romance can be beautifully portrayed by making your own time capsule. Fill a plastic or metal box with items that symbolize your relationship and say something about your personalities. Include your wedding picture and other significant memorabilia of your lives together.

Ceremoniously bury the box in a special place in your backyard. Decorate this area with flowers and shrubs, and keep the area trimmed and neat as a constant reminder of the treasure below. On a future landmark anniversary, dig up the box and relive those early years of your relationship. Or you can leave the box for another generation to dig up.

Memory Lane

♥ The most appreciated gifts are often those you cannot buy. Give your lover an anniversary gift of memories. Plan a quiet evening alone—just you, your spouse, a bottle of champagne, and some old photo albums. Enjoy sitting with your mate as you pore over old pictures and reminisce over times gone by. This walk down memory lane is sure to stir up old feelings and emotions. You'll probably come across some photos that will make you laugh, and others that will make you cry. It is an occasion to share your hopes and fears. No matter what, remembering and sharing past events is a wonderful opportunity for strengthening the bond between you. It is a wonderful way to spend your anniversary together.

Marriage Encounter

After a number of years, many happily married couples get caught up in the everyday ins and outs of their individual lives and begin to lose sight of each other. This is not to say that the couple doesn't love each other or that they are not happy together. What it does mean is that with careers to support, children to raise, a home to maintain, and the never-ending challenges of life to face, a couple is likely to lose the strong passion they once felt as newlyweds.

If you feel that your marriage is in this sort of "humdrum" state of comfortability, you might be interested in attending a Marriage Encounter Weekend. The weekend is run by a team of trained couples and a Catholic priest. You do not have to be Catholic to attend. Marriage Encounter is for any happily married couple regardless of faith, race, age, education, or financial status. The weekend is designed to expand and deepen the joys a couple shares together by showing them special one-on-one communication techniques; these techniques help them to stay focused on each other. The encounter starts with the love you feel for your spouse and helps you to build, expand, and deepen your relationship.

Marriage Encounter is not a professional counseling service. It is not a retreat, nor is it a marriage clinic or sensitivity course. It is not a time to look at the past, but rather a time to look toward your future together. The weekend is a positive, simple, common-sense experience between a husband and wife that revitalizes marriage.

For further information, contact the Worldwide Marriage Encounter at 1-800-795-LOVE.

Romance Revisited

♥ Have you ever felt as young and energetic as you did when you first fell in love? Even the most creative romantic couples can use a little "passion boost" from time to time. Try to recapture some of those wondrous feelings of first love. On your anniversary, take a day and return to a place you frequented in the early years of your relationship. Possible places may include:

☐ Bars.

☐ Beaches.

☐ Bowling alleys.

☐ Cafés.

☐ Dance clubs.

☐ Your former hometown.

☐ Former houses and/or apartments you once lived in.

☐ Parks.

☐ Restaurants.

☐ Roller rinks.

☐ Schools.

☐ Ski resorts.

☐ A college campus.

Message of Lights

♥ Do you want to be grand about your anniversary message of love? Then move it outdoors. Write out your message in large letters cut from styrofoam, then lay out the message on your front lawn. You can further illuminate this message to your spouse by outlining the letters with Christmas lights. Such a message is sure to break up your partner's otherwise routine drive home.

Renew Your Vows

♥ Not counting the preparation snags and the inevitable family disputes, wasn't your wedding day one of the most special ones of your life? If you have been married many years, and the recollections of your life together are warm and loving, you might consider renewing your wedding vows on a special anniversary.

This symbolic act of devotion is something you and your spouse will probably want to plan together. Invite friends and family members who attended your wedding, as well as the member of the clergy who performed the ceremony. Then once again, in front of these loving witnesses, look into each other's eyes and exchange your vows of love and fidelity.

Second Proposals

♥ Did you have one of those fairy-tale marriage proposals, or was it a little more down to earth? Regardless of the nature of your proposal, it was a means of reaffirming and strengthening your commitment to each other. Consider making a second proposal to remind your spouse of your love. Here are a few ideas:

❑ In the middle of the night, climb a ladder up to the bedroom window and propose to your spouse all over again (if your bedroom is not on an upper floor, improvise). You might accompany your proposal with a bouquet of flowers, or have a guitarist strumming love songs at the base of the ladder.

❑ Bring back days gone by by making your second proposal during a horse-and-buggy ride. As an added touch, bring along some taped music and a bottle of champagne.

❑ Use balloons to frame your second proposal. Inflate as many balloons of the same color as you can, and fill her favorite room with them. Write a note requesting your spouse's hand in marriage again and place it in a balloon of a different color.

You might also choose to include a ring in this balloon. Inflate the balloon and bury it under the others. Leave your spouse a clue as to where the anniversary gift is, or perhaps tape a pin inside the anniversary card.

Special Dinner Touches

♥ Taking your spouse out for an anniversary dinner at a special restaurant is a nice way to say you love him or her, no question about it; however, you could do things to make this a more memorable event. For starters, you might send your spouse a formal invitation for the anniversary dinner, along with a gift or some roses. Proceed to stop at the restaurant on your way home from work and let the staff know of the importance of the evening. Have the table decorated with roses and candles. If possible, arrange to have a musician or two serenade you. Have the waiter serve your spouse a small gift at the end of the meal. Have chilled champage waiting for your arrival home, and end the day with a toast to your wonderful life together.

A Special Night Out

♥ For your anniversary, go somewhere special, somewhere out of the norm. A dinner theater or a comedy club can provide a very full and entertaining night. Or you could get tickets for the ballet, a symphony, a play, or a musical revue. If you rarely do these types of things, it will mark the anniversary as unique and memorable.

Wedding Song

♥ Every couple has a special wedding song that they dance to during their wedding reception. An anniversary seems like a natural time to introduce this song in a unique setting. Take your spouse out to dinner at a fancy restaurant that has a piano player or other form of live musical entertainment. Arrange to have your wedding song played while you are celebrating with your spouse. Take your partner's hand and lead him or her to the dance floor where you can, once again, dance to your wedding song.

A Wedding Reunion

For a thoughtful anniversary gift, bring together some special people from your wedding day—those you haven't seen in a long while—for a heartfelt reunion. This is a thoughtful, wonderful gesture that will be appreciated by all. Or plan a visit with the priest, minister, or rabbi who performed your wedding ceremony. Update him or her with the many changes that have occurred since you last met.

Final Romantic Thoughts on Anniversaries

Whether you have been married for one year or fifty, your wedding anniversary is a day to honor your lifelong bond of love. Be sure to take time out from your busy schedule to plan a romantic celebration. This is the perfect opportunity to let your partner know how much your time together has meant to you, how important your marriage is, and how much you are looking forward to your future.

4. *Having a Baby*

A baby is the ultimate expression of a couple's love. Not much else can compare to the creation of a life; a living, breathing, work of art that is the product of your coupling. How incredibly romantic!

The very nature of this miracle cries out for a celebration. If you are an expectant mother, you can use the discovery of your pregnancy as cause to rejoice, and maybe come up with a clever, creative way to break the news to the baby's father. If you are an expectant father, you can use this good news as a well-justified reason to do something extra special for the mother-to-be.

When you discover that you are expecting, have some fun with baby-related affairs. This chapter provides you with a number of touching and, yes, romantic suggestions for both expectant parents and new ones. Remember that the addition of a baby into your lives does not mean an end to the romance you share. The birth of your baby will bring the love you feel for each other to a new and different level.

IDEAS FOR ANNOUNCING YOUR PREGNANCY

Often, both partners are very much involved in discovering the results of their pregnancy test. On the other hand, some women choose to make the discovery on their own and wait for just the right moment to break the news to their partners. If you fall into this last category, one of the following creative news-breaking suggestions may be just right for you.

Flower Power

♥ Never underestimate the power of a bloom. Here is one way that a floral arrangement can be used to alert your partner to your pregnancy. Send him a bouquet of pink and blue flowers. To each pink bloom, attach a card with a girl's name on it. Attach boy's names to the blue flowers. Be sure that baby's breath is included in the bouquet. It shouldn't take him long to figure out this floral message.

Spreading the News

♥ There are many creative ways to get the the message of your pregnancy to the father of your child. Check out the following suggestions:

❒ If your partner frequents a restaurant or tavern, and you know he is going to be there for lunch, have the manager write out the announcement on the "daily specials" board.

❒ Rent a portable road sign and display your message somewhere along your partner's usual route home.

❒ Take out a classified ad in your partner's favorite newspaper for your announcement. You might consider highlighting or circling the ad so he doesn't miss it.

❒ Get hold of your partner's daily newspaper before he has had a chance to read it. Write out the news of your pregnancy on a piece of paper, then tape it somewhere in his favorite newspaper section. For example, if he is an avid reader of the sports section, your announcement might state that there will be a new athlete in the family. If he prefers the entertainment section, your note can allude to a new star on the rise.

❏ Write a letter to your partner as if it were from the baby. Using crayons, draw a simple picture of the two of you holding a baby.

❏ Get a copy of a baby magazine like *Parents*, then hide it in the newspaper for him to discover. Prepare to play dumb if he asks how it got there. Reveal your news only if he concludes that you are pregnant.

Dinner Talk

❤ Many people like to announce important news over dinner. Here are some unique twists to this idea:

❏ Plan a special Chinese-style dinner (either at home or at a restaurant). Slip the news of your pregnancy into a fortune cookie. If you are dining in a restaurant, make arrangements for the waiter to give your partner the special fortune cookie.

❏ This idea gets extra points for being cute. Plan to have dinner with your husband at a restaurant. Beforehand, make arrangements with your waiter to serve your partner his drink in a baby bottle. See how long it takes your mate to catch on. Or have the waiter bring a covered dish to your partner. When he lifts the cover from his plate, have him discover a jar of baby food.

❏ Plan to have dinner in a restaurant that offers singing entertainment. If possible, arrange to have the singer announce your pregnancy through a song.

Tricky Tricks

❤ Consider having your good news announced to your partner with a standard balloon-o-gram or telegram. Or try making your announcement in one of the following tricky ways:

❑ Present your husband with a book of names. Highlight your favorite choices, and add your last name to them.

❑ Draw your family tree, and put a question mark where your child's name is supposed to go. This is a nice way of announcing that a new name will be added soon.

❑ If a pregnancy test strip has let you know that you are pregnant, why not let it tell your husband too? Hide the strip in a romantic greeting card or even a Father's Day card. (It will be quite a surprise for your partner to receive a Father's Day card when you don't have children of your own—yet.)

❑ Purchase a baby album. On the first page, attach your positive pregnancy strip, or perhaps a note from your doctor confirming your pregnancy. After wrapping the gift in baby paper, present it to your partner.

Hint Hint

♥ Being sneaky has never been so much fun. Let your husband discover your new-found secret through some well-placed clues. Here are a few ideas:

❑ Do you indicate important upcoming events on your calendar? Mark the baby's due date on your calendar and attach a baby picture to that day. Nonchalantly ask your partner to look something up that takes place during that month. When he scans the calendar he will notice your clever "announcement."

❑ Want a real eye-catching (and expensive) way to tell your partner of your pregnancy? Hire an airplane to pull a banner that announces your good news.

❑ Place a pillow under your shirt to look as if you are nine months pregnant. Then approach your partner and say, "Hi honey. Guess what."

Baby Talk

♥ Buy or make a card that is blank inside. Write and/or print the word "baby" in many different languages. Upon opening the card, your partner will probably be confused. After he translates one or two of the words (*bambino* is usually a tip-off), he will likely get the message. The following is a list of foreign words for "baby."

Language	Word for Baby	Pronunciation
Danish	spædbarn	SPAID-barn
French	bébé	bay-BAY
German	kindlein	KINNT-line
Greek	moró	more-OH
Hebrew	tinok	ti-NOK
Italian	bambino	bahm-BEE-noh
Japanese	akanboo	ah-KAN-bow
Norwegian	spebarn	spe-BARN
Portuguese	bebé	beh-BEH
Russian	rebyonok	reb-YO-nuk
Spanish	criatura	kry-a-TOO-rah
Swahili	taz	TAHZ
Swedish	spädbarn	SPAID-barn
Yiddish	oyfele	OY-feh-leh
Irish	bunók	bu-NOK

Caught in the Clutter

♥ If your husband's work area is constantly covered in notes, use this to your advantage. Write a note that states the news of your pregnancy, or one that tells your spouse that he is about to be a father. Place the note (or notes) somewhere amidst the clutter of his office—on his desk, on the wall, or tacked to his bulletin board.

Lullaby Songs

♥ Make a tape with lots of songs that include the word "baby." Try to give your partner the subliminal message of your pregnancy by playing this tape often. Have it on during dinner or while your partner is getting ready for work. You can secretly put the tape in the car's tape deck and have it ready to play as soon as he turns on the ignition. It will be interesting to see how long it takes your partner to figure out what's going on.

Here are a few song ideas for your tape:

❒ "Baby Baby" by Amy Grant
❒ "Danny's Song" by Loggins and Messina
❒ "Blue Eyes" by Elton John
❒ "Baby You Can Drive My Car" by the Beatles
❒ "Having My Baby" by Paul Anka
❒ "Baby Love" by the Supremes
❒ "Babe" by Styx
❒ "Baby I'm a Want You" by Bread
❒ "Stepping Out With My Baby" by Fred Astaire

Say It With Movies

♥ Plan a stay-at-home movie night. Offer to go to the video store alone, then come back with a few movies, all with baby-related themes. He'll probably figure out that something is up as he reads through the titles. After that, it probably won't be long before he realizes what you are trying to tell him through your movie choices.

The following movies are good choices:

❏ *Three Men and a Baby*

❏ *Baby Boom*

❏ *Look Who's Talking*

❏ *Look Who's Talking, Too*

❏ *Look Who's Talking Now*

❏ *She's Having a Baby*

❏ *Penny Serenade*

❏ *The First Time*

❏ *A Global Affair*

❏ *Blondie's Blessed Event*

❏ *For Heaven's Sake*

IDEAS FOR EXPECTANT FATHERS

This is an ideal time to show the mother of your future child a little extra tenderness and affection. The physical and emotional changes that occur in a pregnant woman can cause her to become extra sensitive and emotional. It is the perfect time for you to show her your unconditional love and support.

The Morning Watch

♥ Many pregnant women experience bouts of morning sickness during their first trimester. If your partner is one of these women, a little extra consideration from you might help her tolerate this difficult time.

Many pregnant women find that eating a cracker or two will settle a queasy stomach. Go to the grocery store and purchase several different varieties of crackers. Place all of the cracker boxes in one large box. Then wrap the box in cheerful paper and tie it up with a big bow. This expression of your understanding may be just what your partner needs. It is also a reminder of how thoughtful and loving you are.

Food Fetish

♥ Passionate and outrageous food cravings are common among pregnant women. Anyone who knows a woman who has had a baby can attest to the often bizarre nature of these food desires. It can be a nice gesture for you to quietly observe the nature of her cravings, then use this information to feed her passion. Periodically surprise her with super-size quantities of her "food lust" (maybe along with a couple of her favorite magazines). This is just a little thing, a gesture of love, that shows her your awareness of the changes that her body is going through.

Make Her Feel Beautiful

♥ Many pregnant women feel fat and unattractive, especially during the third trimester. Be sensitive to these feelings and constantly remind your partner how beautiful she is to you. Oh, and another thing, for obvious reasons, try not to verbally admire any thin, attractive women you see on television.

Maternity Massages

♥ One of the more notable discomforts in a woman's body as her pregnancy advances is muscle ache. Her back, feet, neck, and just about any other part of her body can feel aches and pains. As a gesture of your affection, offer to massage her aching body part. She will appreciate your effort to make her feel better.

ROMANTIC IDEAS FOR NEW PARENTS

If you are a new parent, you are probably already aware of a new kind of love in your heart. Never before have you felt a love so precious and tender as the one you feel when you look at your newborn child. And the new bond of love and respect you feel for your partner is equally priceless. The following ideas are suggestions for expressing this appreciation you feel for your mate.

Mother and Child

♥ There is probably no stronger bond than the one between a mother and child; it is possibly the purest form of love. A terribly romantic and considerate action for a father to take is to commission a portrait of his wife and child. This is a timeless gift that can be handed down to future generations.

A Storybook Treasure

♥ Sentimental gifts are always appreciated. Present your partner with a hardcover version of her favorite children's story, fairy tale, or collection of nursery rhymes. Make sure to write a personal inscription to her on the first page and date it. Both you and your partner can enjoy reading to your child from this book, which just may turn out to be his or her favorite, too. This treasured gift is one that can be enjoyed for generations.

Word Power

♥ One way to let the mother of your child know how much she means to you is through the written word. Compose your own song or poem, or simply write her a letter that conveys how special she and the baby are to you. You can have your precious words framed before presenting them to your love. What a beautiful keepsake.

Welcome Home

♥ The difficulties of childbirth are legendary. Such a sacrifice is definitely worthy of recognition. Let your partner know how much it means to you by celebrating her return home with your child. Make it a welcome home like never before. Decorate the house with banners, balloons, streamers, pink or blue flowers, children's toys, pictures made with crayons, etc., all of which say how much you love your wife and the ultimate gift that she has brought home to be part of your family—your baby. You can make your wife feel extra special by picking her and the baby up from the hospital in a limousine (don't forget to bring an infant safety seat with you). Have the house ready for her return—clean, of course—and make sure her favorite pajamas are ready for her. If she is exhausted (which is very likely), let her sleep, with the promise that you will care for the baby while she rests. You may also want to leave flowers on her pillow for her as a pleasant surprise.

A Parallel Life

♥ The really special thing about the birth of a child is that it is the creation of a new life that you can help to shape and watch unfold. One meaningful way to celebrate the birth of your child is to plant a tree. Soon after your child is born, you and your spouse can plant a small seedling in a special place. Nurture it and watch it grow with your child. This is a living monument to your love that can also be something unique and personal to your child.

Baby's Book

♥ Collecting pictures and mementos is one of the most common ways of expressing how much the people in your life mean to you. A baby, which is the most wonderful result of a romantic relationship, definitely deserves such a collection. A baby book can be a treasured and useful reference for both parents and child in later years. So get together with your spouse and construct a thorough and delightful baby book that records your child's birth, growth, and development. Include information like the day the baby was conceived (if you know); keepsakes like the hospital bracelet, your baby's footprint, a birth announcement, a lock of hair, and notes or a mention of gifts sent by family and friends; information about important "firsts" (baby's first smile, first laugh, first step, first words, etc.), the baby's baptism or other religious ceremonies, illnesses, and important events; a family tree; and special photographs. This can be compiled in a regular photo album or scrapbook, or you can buy a readymade baby book and just fill in the information. The important thing is to do it together—and to use this activity to help you enjoy this unique time in your lives.

Special Vintage

♥ Wine is intrinsically linked with romance. Just think of how many times you have seen a couple drinking wine over a special romantic dinner in movies. You can use wine in a slightly different way to celebrate your child's birth. Buy a bottle of *premier cru* (first growth) Bordeaux wine (also known as claret) from the year of the baby's birth. Choose wine from one of the five famous chateaus of Bordeaux (Latour, Margaux, Lafite-Rothschild, Mouton-Rothschild, or Haut-Brion) or another noteworthy wine. The Bordeaux make outstanding wines that are well suited for the purpose because they age splendidly. Good vintages age well for 50 to 100 years and become rare and valuable as they grow older. These wines are not inexpensive—be prepared to spend $75 to $150 per bottle—and they must be stored in a cool dark place, such as in the basement near the floor. After a number of years, you and your spouse can have an unusual romantic dinner that celebrates a special time in your lives with a bottle of fine wine from the year your baby was born.

A Positive Change

♥ The birth of a child causes many changes in a relationship. It really is stunning how far-reaching this influence is on your lives. On the one hand, a child can be the single greatest plus to a relationship. It can bind you and your mate together like nothing else; instead of being just a couple, you are now a family. This can really make you look at your priorities again. However, a child's presence can also challenge the strength of your relationship. For the sake of your relationship, it is important to remain positive and to approach this change in your lives with hope and teamwork. Remember, if you or your spouse is feeling stressed out, romance and feelings of love will be the furthest things from your mind. Below are listed a number of things to keep in mind after having a child that will help keep your connection to your spouse close and allow your love to flourish.

❑ Pay attention when help is needed. Getting the housework done when you have a new baby can seem like a distant dream. Fathers might try to do more than their usual share of domestic work for a period.

❑ Take special pains to be unselfish and to be there for your spouse. Cut back on time spent away from home. Try to be more aware than ever of your spouse's feelings and concerns, and be supportive. Consideration of your spouse will be especially appreciated at this time.

❑ Try to share both the burdens and joys of parenthood. If you feel that child care is solely your responsibility, it is easy to become exhausted and to begin feeling resentful. Conversely, if your spouse assumes sole responsibility for child care, you can start to feel "left out" or ignored. In either case, your relationship can suffer. The happiest families are those in which the parents have a strong bond with each other, and each of them has a strong bond with their children.

❑ Focus on the small things. Try to compliment your spouse regularly, maybe about the way he or she handled a situation with the baby. When your spouse does something for you, express your appreciation in words. As much as possible, try not to think of your own needs and problems, but of those of your spouse and child—your family.

❐ Make time to be alone together. No matter how hectic your lives have become, find a short period of time every day to be with each other and "reconnect." From time to time, ask a family member or a friend to help out so that you can meet for lunch or dinner or go see a movie—just the two of you.

Final Romantic Thoughts on Having a Baby

Having a baby together is the ultimate expression of your love. Use this time in your lives to enjoy each other and to marvel at the life you have created. If you are an expectant mother who finds out about your pregnancy first, this is a great opportunity to surprise your mate. And if you are a new or expectant father, what better time is there to let your wife know how much she and your new baby mean to you? A baby is a perfect excuse for you to spoil and pamper your mate.

5. Christmas

Christmas is a most wonderful and exciting time of the year. It also is a time that reflects the dualism of the holidays—the fact that there are two or more sides to all things. Christmas has come to be a larger-than-life event filled with presents, food, and parties. But underneath this is a deeper, more spiritual aspect that gives true meaning to all the celebration.

The true Christmas spirit is very important. Most of us lead busy and hectic lives, with seemingly too many demands on our time and too many economic pressures that govern our actions. As a result, the unseen side of Christmas, with its focus on the gifts of love, family, sharing, support, and faith, is more necessary now than ever.

Christmas can be a model for showing the important, but often unspoken, aspects of our lives that really deserve to be in the spotlight more often. Faith and love go together in deserving a prominent place and special attention, and there is no time like Christmas to help us see this.

ROMANTIC CHRISTMAS GIFTS

Christmas is the most important gift-giving time of the year, so naturally, some of the most romantic Christmas ideas involve ways to make or present a gift. Most of these ideas can also easily be combined with other romantic plans for the holidays.

A Christmas Character Presentation

♥ The unwrapping of gifts can be a very entertaining part of the entire gift-giving process. Making the unwrapping a bit difficult and puzzling adds to the fun. One way to do this is to make a large Christmas character such as Frosty, Rudolph, the Grinch, or Santa Claus out of papier-mâché and seal your gift inside. As you work on the figure, be sure to leave a large enough hole in the bottom for your gift to fit through. Once the figure has dried, insert the gift and seal over the hole with more papier-mâché. Then paint the character and add a bow and a card to your creation. Check your local library for how-to books on creating papier-mâché figures.

On Christmas morning (or whenever you and your sweetheart exchange presents), act as if the character is your gift. In your card write a riddle or clues to lead to discovery of the gift inside the character. In subsequent years, you can use your creative "gift wrap" as a Christmas decoration.

Christmas Coupons

♥ We have used this idea in earlier chapters, but maybe you haven't yet. Gift certificates for different tasks or activities make great stocking stuffers for Christmas. You can modify the coupons to reflect Christmas favors and tasks. Some ideas for Christmas coupons are:

❑ Put away the Christmas decorations.

❑ Clean up after a Christmas party.

❑ Attend the Christmas concert, play, or other performance of your choice.

❑ Help bake Christmas cookies and other desserts.

❑ Watch the Christmas movie of your choice.

❑ Attend the Christmas party of your choice.

❑ Spend the time to shop for gifts for mutual friends.

❑ Write and send Christmas cards.

❑ Help put up Christmas decorations.

It is a good idea to mix these in with coupons for other, more personal "services" your mate would enjoy (see page 12 for suggestions).

Christmas Garden

♥ Christmas is a time for spiritual growth. And what better symbolizes growth than a garden? Exercise your creative talents and make an indoor garden with a Christmas theme. Use Christmas plants such as poinsettias and hollies (for a truly miniature garden, check your local nursery or garden center for dwarf varieties of these plants), and decorate the garden with small items such as candles, nativity scene figures, angels, stars, snowmen, Santa Claus figurines, candy canes, and other holiday goodies. If your garden is small enough, you can put it in a basket or bowl; if it's a little larger, you can use a large flowerpot or planter. You can do this every year using a different theme.

Christmas Photos

♥ Christmas is also a time for taking lots of pictures. Cameras are rarely as visible as during family gatherings from December 24 to January 1. Use color copies of photographs from past celebrations and winters to create a gift (have your local copy center make laser copies from your original color photos). There are a couple of ways that you can make use of these pictures:

❐   Create a witty story or comic strip about Christmas or an actual Christmas incident. Paste captions on or below the pictures. It's a good idea to review all of the past photos before you begin; you might notice a common thread that can be the basis for your story.

❐   Create a chronological collage of all those happy Christmas moments. Or, if it is a struggle to get distant family members together every year, create a Christmas scene with all the family members present. This idea also looks nice in black and white, for a more classic look to be saved for years to come.

A Classic Christmas Romance

♥   Christmas has inspired many classic stories and fairy tales. Use this inspiration to create your own Christmas story to give as a gift. Select one of these stories or fairy tales and make it your own by substituting yourself, your partner, and your family and friends for the characters in the story. This is another gift that serves nicely as a family keepsake.

A Favorite Toy

♥   A favorite toy from your spouse's childhood makes a gift that can rekindle old memories and show how much you care. Either purchase a toy similar to the adored toy, or go to your mate's parents' home and find the very one your loved one clung to as a best friend in youth. Some clever investigating may be required to track down the cherished plaything.

Make A Christmas Bauble

♥   Many people are passionate about Christmas ornaments. Some people collect them all year round, and some possess ornaments that have been with them since childhood. The following are ideas for ways you can use Christmas ornaments to express your romantic feelings for your lover:

❏ Buy a clear plastic ornament ball from a crafts store and place a romantic picture of the two of you, or the entire family, inside. Decorate the ornament with lace, ribbons, holly, dried heather, and rosebuds.

❏ Buy some plain ornaments and decorate them yourself using acrylic paints. Write a short Christmas message or a romantic thought on the ornament with a calligraphy marker.

❏ Each year you and your love are together, buy or make each other a unique ornament to add to the collection.

❏ If you have a creative streak, make an original ornament as a gift. This can look however you wish it to. The key is to make it uniquely personal. One idea is to use small items or images that remind you of your partner and the times you have spent together. Another idea is to use little trinkets from your spouse's childhood for the basic elements.

Stuff a Stocking

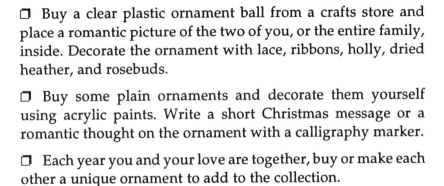 Another Christmas tradition is that of the stocking. To create special Christmas memories, choose a romantic theme for your stocking stuffers. Items you can include are new lingerie, perfume, sexy photos of yourself, romance novels, chocolate, coupons for love (see page 12), a CD of your partner's favorite love songs, dried or fresh flowers, a book of romantic poetry, massage lotion, and a love letter.

Another option is to sew a Christmas stocking yourself. You can decorate the outside however you like, using ribbons, sequins, beads, bits of fake fur, shapes cut out of felt, or anything else, to create romantic images, Christmas scenes, or an abstract design—or just to write your lover's name. Stuff the stocking with as many things as you can, including a nice

Wrapping It All Up

How you present your gift is just as important as the gift itself. Since you have taken the time to select something special for your partner, be sure to put some thought into the way you give your gift. Be inventive with your choice of wrapping. Use your partner's favorite color; adorn the gift with a flower, an ornament, lace, or decorative stickers. After all, the first thing your partner will notice is the way your gift is wrapped. We have included here some ideas for creative gift wrapping, as well as some ideas for hiding special gifts.

❑ *Make a decoupage gift box and put your gift inside.*

❑ *Put your gift on a new stuffed animal.*

❑ *Put your gift in the pocket of a new shirt or jacket.*

❑ *Put jewelry in a new jewelry box or jewelry travel pouch.*

❑ *Place your gift inside a new pocketbook or wallet.*

❑ *Hide your gift inside a new Christmas ornament.*

❑ *Wrap your gift in plain brown paper with an extravagant bow.*

❑ *Put a ring in a champagne glass.*

❑ *Freeze your gift in an ice cube and place it in his or her drink.*

❑ *Hang your gift from a Christmas tree branch or a new plant.*

❑ *Hide tickets in the appropriate month of a new calendar.*

❑ *Hide your gift in his or her car, then wrap the car with a giant bow.*

❑ *Hide your gift in a gingerbread or chocolate house.*

❑ *Put your gift in a small box, then put that box in a larger box, then put that box in a larger box.*

❑ *Wrap your gift in lace or silk.*

❑ *Tie a small gift to the ribbon on a wrapped box and tuck it into the bow.*

❑ *Wrap your gift in a silk scarf and tie it with lace.*

❑ *Hide a small gift inside the bud of a flower.*

❑ *Hide your gift in a gift basket of scented lotions and soaps.*

❑ *Hide vacation tickets in a new travel bag.*

variety of small, silly items along with more meaningful gifts. Even (or perhaps especially) if you are not experienced in the ways of needle and thread, your efforts will be greatly appreciated. Again, the personal touch is what matters.

Christmas Cards

When you have worked extra hard to personalize your gift, it deserves a special card to complete it. Here are a few suggestions for a one-of-a-kind Christmas card:

❑ Create a romantic card by using poems or songs with a religious silhouette in the background. Then write a message to tie in the true meaning of Christmas with your feelings about your relationship.

☐ Construct a giant card in the shape of a Christmas character. Decorate the card with wrapping paper, parts of old Christmas cards, photographs, words to Christmas songs, or drawings by your children.

☐ Create a humorous card using fold-outs or cutout windows of Christmas characters and scenes. Do your own drawings, or cut and paste comics or parts of old Christmas cards.

☐ Create a card using color copies of photographs of Christmases past (most copy centers can make good-quality, economical laser copies from your original color photos). One idea is to write warm, reflective comments below each picture. Another is to have a photograph on the front of the card and the punchline or the message inside.

☐ Try to obtain a baby picture of your mate, and use this as the cover for your card or as an inside illustration. For instance, on the outside of the card, you might write, "All I want for Christmas..." and on the inside, under the picture, "...is you." This is sure to warm your lover's heart.

OTHER ROMANTIC CHRISTMAS IDEAS

Christmas is more than exchanging gifts. It is also a time to focus on the joy that comes from loving, and being loved by, the special people in our lives. And it is an excellent time for romance to flourish! This section includes some ideas to add a romantic touch to your Christmas preparations and celebrations.

A Charlie Brown Tree

♥ Picking a Christmas tree from a city lot can be too much like going to a flea market, and tends to be considered more of a hassle than a fun or romantic event. To get into the Christmas spirit, drive out to the country to a tree farm where you and your lover can cut your own tree (many newspapers publish lists or carry advertising that will enable you to find such a place). Make a Charlie Brown-style adventure of it, and carefully pick the perfect tree. Make this part of a package of romantic Christmas activities.

In the spirit of Charlie Brown, make your own ornaments. Use construction paper, or string popcorn and/or cranberries together. Do this while watching Christmas shows on television or listening to Christmas music. You can add a delightfully different touch to your tree by using some natural decorations. Pine cones, for instance, make beautiful ornaments when dried and tied to the branches with red and green ribbons.

Another great activity for pine-cone collectors is making a wreath. Many people enjoy creating decorations on their own, but this is a project that a couple can enjoy together. You can make your Christmas wreath from natural objects, like pine cones, dried grapevines, corn cobs, cedar rope, and holly. With this project you will accomplish two things: You will create a personalized and unique decoration to show the world, and you will spend valuable, creative time with someone you love.

Christmas Celebrations

♥ Some people claim to hate Christmas because of all the stress and busyness it brings. This is a shame, because if you have this attitude, you will miss out on many heartwarming and meaningful experiences. The events and activities of the Christmas season not only are uplifting and soul-satisfying, but also create feelings that spill over into your relationship with your loved one. Don't miss this opportunity to elevate and magnify your love for each other! There are so many activities that surround Christmas, and all you have to do is take advantage of them to get in some time for romance. Here are some ideas to get into a romantic Christmas spirit:

❐ Attend a Christmas concert or pageant together.

❐ Attend midnight services together on Christmas Eve.

❐ Attend a Christmas play together.

❏ Go Christmas carolling together with family and friends.

❏ Bake your own Christmas cookies and desserts together.

❏ Make Christmas crafts together.

❏ Rent Christmas movies. Some ideas are *A Christmas Song, It's a Wonderful Life, Miracle on 34th Street, The Holly and the Ivy, Lilies of the Field, One Magic Christmas, The Muppets Christmas Carol,* and *The Santa Clause.*

❏ Watch a pile of kids' specials with the entire family.

❏ Go ice-skating together, or with the entire family, preferably at an outdoor rink or frozen pond or lake.

❏ Visit friends and relatives.

❏ Take a horse and buggy (or sleigh) ride.

❏ Decorate your home and wrap gifts together.

You may notice that the trick to adding romance to these activities is to do them *together.* This will give you some relaxing time to spend with each other and to share your dreams, memories, and deepest feelings.

Christmas Habitat

♥ Don't be a Scrooge—get in the spirit! Christmas is a friendly time of the year. It is a time for visiting, giving, and celebrating, three things that will put you in a joyous mood that can spread into your relationship with your lover. You can create a constant reminder of this spiritual season by decorating your home. This is simple and fun to do, and, most important, it can be done together. Ideas for decorations include the following:

❏ Paper or felt cutouts.

❏ Cloth hangings.

❏ Papier-mâché Christmas characters.

❏ Candles.

❑ Bells.

❑ Angels.

❑ Stars.

❑ Snowmen.

❑ Santa Claus and/or elves.

❑ A homemade popcorn and cranberry garland.

❑ Christmas stockings.

❑ Candy canes.

❑ Nativity scenes.

❑ Reindeer.

❑ That most important element for romance . . . mistletoe.

Christmas Music

♥ Record or purchase a cassette tape of seasonal music that the two of you can enjoy while decorating the Christmas tree, baking cookies, or wrapping gifts. If you tape it yourself, you can include the music that the two of you like the best. It it is easy to get yourself in the Christmas spirit this way. Anticipation helps to bring the magic of Christmas to life.

Favorite Christmas Stories

♥ One of the great traditions of this time of year is a literary one. There are numerous books that deal with different aspects of the Christmas season. A pleasant romantic activity can include the reading of Dickens' *A Christmas Carol* or another favorite story of the season that reminds you of the meaning behind Christmas. At the end of the day, relax and read to each other—around a warm fire, with eggnog and roasted chestnuts, if possible. If you have children, include them in this activity. This makes a wonderful Christmas tradition that can help weave meaning and value into the holiday.

The Christmas Tree of Love

♥ Make a personalized Christmas tree for your lover. Buy a small potted fir tree, and decorate the pot with red and green paint, paper, or anything else along traditional Christmas lines. Cut out paper ornaments and hang them on the branches. For an especially pleasing touch, write love messages on the ornaments, such as reasons why you love your partner, private jokes, meaningful quotes, a dinner invitation, or sexy messages. Another great idea is to put personal pictures on the ornaments. Hang candy on the branches as well. This idea has added meaning because plants represent growth—in this case, the growth of your love.

Twelve Days of Christmas

♥ "On the first day of Christmas, my true love gave to me . . ." Bring this old song to life with your Christmas offering. Two ideas come immediately to mind with the "twelve days" theme.

The first idea is to purchase twelve gifts for your lover. Mix small, fun gifts with more serious, romantic ones, and give one gift each day. If you want to give the final gift on Christmas day, give the first one on December 14; otherwise, give the first of the twelve gifts on Christmas morning and continue until January 5. That way, even though the rest of the world may think Christmas is over, it will still be Christmas for you and your lover! You can employ friends and family to help work out interesting presentations over the course of the twelve days.

The second idea is to give twelve of one item, eleven of another, ten of another, and so on, until you reach a single, final gift. Use things like candy canes, kisses, or gift certificates for the performance of household chores for the gifts of larger numbers of items. (This idea can also be easily modified for Hanukkah by using the number theme of eight.) Have some fun with this one!

The Unconventional Mistletoe

Liberally hang sprigs of mistletoe throughout your home and use your imagination when you meet your lover beneath the magical plant. One idea is to gift-wrap the bottom half of a box, and fill the box with slips of paper on which you've written down different romantic acts. Each time you meet under the mistletoe, let your lover pull out one folded slip from the box. This way, there will be an element of wonder and anticipation every time there is a chance meeting under the mistletoe. Your lover will look forward to each new encounter. (Just remember, if this game is for your partner's eyes only, you will want to put it away when company comes!) The following is a list of ideas for under-the-mistletoe offerings to choose from:

❑ Give a traditional kiss.

❑ Give a passionate kiss.

❑ Give a long hug.

❑ Express loving words from the bottom of your heart.

❑ Give a shoulder and neck massage.

❑ Do a slow dance.

❑ Give a feast of chocolates (hide them nearby).

❑ Make love.

❑ Give a small gift (hide it nearby).

❑ Kiss your lover's hand.

❑ Sing a short line or phrase.

❑ Present a funny or loving Christmas card (hide it nearby).

❑ Promise to do something you have been putting off.

❑ Hug your lover and whisper sweet words into his or her ear.

❑ Hug and kiss your spouse all over his or her face.

❑ Hug your lover and give "love bites" on his or her neck and earlobes.

Final Romantic Thoughts on Christmas

The Christmas season brings with it feelings of warmth and caring. This time of year presents an ideal atmosphere for romance. Whether you put time aside to decorate your tree together, to bake cookies together, or even to brave the shopping crowds together, the spirit of love and giving will be in the air—enjoy it!

6. New Year's Celebrations

Whether you are staying at home or are going to a big holiday bash, New Year's Eve is one holiday that simply sizzles with excitement and romance! There is an aura of mystery and anticipation that surrounds this holiday because of the year to come. Use this electrically charged holiday as a chance to get closer to the one you love.

The possibilities for New Year's Eve romance are endless, but New Year's Day can prove to be just as rewarding. This is a time to reminisce about the year that has just passed, and to think about how you handled last year's resolutions. You also have a whole year ahead of you to think about, and the two of you can do this together. Romance is in the air for any holiday that allows you to sit back and quietly share your plans for the future with the one you love. You can plan all of the wonderful things the two of you want to do in years to come, or simply dream out loud.

So stock up on noisemakers, and get ready for romance.

ROMANTIC IDEAS FOR NEW YEAR'S EVE

New Year's Eve is a holiday that has long been associated with finding love and romance. Whether you prefer celebrating out with a crowd or quietly at home, this section offers ideas for adding a distinctive, romantic feeling to the festivities.

Take to the Air

♥ Watch the New Year's ball drop from a different angle. If the weather permits, take a helicopter or hot air ballon ride over the area where the ball drops. This is an original way of spending time with your partner, and it is one New Year's Eve you won't soon forget. You can look in your local telephone directory for a company that offers these charter services.

Celebrity Treatment

♥ If you like to go out on New Year's Eve, but you want to spend the night with only that special someone, take your lover out in style. Rent a limousine for the evening. To add a little mystery to your plans, send a formal invitation with a single rose to your partner, asking him or her to be ready and waiting to be picked up at a certain time, but without specifying your destination. Then the evening is all yours. Have dinner at a romantic restaurant, go dancing, or just ride around in luxury sipping champagne. To end your perfect evening, find a quiet spot, like a scenic overlook, to ring in the new year. (Just be sure to make any necessary reservations, such as for the limousine or restaurant, well in advance.)

For Homebodies

♥ If you and your mate prefer to spend this holiday alone, make the evening a romantic one. Prepare a special dinner together, with all of the fixings. Make sure to use candles, music, and flowers to create atmosphere. Dress up for each other—just because you are staying home, that doesn't mean that blue jeans are proper attire. Let this be an occasion for a formal, intimate party for two. You may want to conclude your evening with some slow dancing by candlelight while waiting to ring in the new year.

A variation on this idea is to have your dinner catered. Have a private formal dinner, but let someone else do the cooking. There are companies that will bring in dinner for you, right down to the table linens and silverware. Check your local telephone directory under "Caterers" for these services.

A New Year's Surprise

If you want to make this holiday a special one alone with your lover, plan a surprise. While your partner is out of the house, fill the place with balloons. Break out the champagne, light some candles, and put on some romantic music. Change into something special for the occasion, and lay out an outfit for your lover. Or, if you do not live together, decorate your place with romantic touches, and send an invitation, along with some flowers, to your lover. Specify whether he or she should dress formally or casually, and what time he or she will be expected to arrive. The rest is up to you!

A Theme Year

If you like to throw parties, but want to add a new twist to the ordinary snacks and champagne, throw a theme party. An idea that is especially appropriate for New Year's, when we observe the passage of the old year and the start of the new, is to pick a year or decade from the past for your theme. For instance, you could pick the Roaring Twenties, and offer your guests the option of coming in twenties attire. Do a little research on whatever period you choose to help you select the the appropriate food and drinks to serve, and decorate properly. For a Roaring Twenties theme, you could transform your home into a speakeasy. Other themes that make for great parties include a tropical island, a casino, a masquerade party, romantic literary figures, storybook characters, or anything else your mind conjures up.

Double New Year's

♥ Celebrating with friends is a wonderful way to ring in the new year, but if you're out at a party, a moment for a kiss at midnight may be all the time you have to be alone with your special someone. To make your own New Year's romance, prepare a second post-party celebration. Leave a bottle of champagne in the refrigerator and party hats and streamers near the television before you go out. Then, when you come home, break out the champagne, put on the party hats, and celebrate all over again. If you live in the Eastern, Central, or Mountain time zone, you can even catch the beginning of the new year on television—in California. Many stations carry coverage of New Year's in California 1:00, 2:00, or 3:00 A.M. (depending on where you live). If you live on the West Coast, or if you can't find coverage of the California celebrations on television, you can always set your videocassette recorder to tape the local New Year's festivities while you are out enjoying them elsewhere. When you get home, cuddle up for a private celebration!

The Picnic

♥ A picnic on New Year's? Why not? Actually, this idea can be used for either New Year's Eve or New Year's Day.
If you don't like a lot of fanfare on this holiday, have a simple celebration. Remember, simple things are often the most romantic! Spread out a picnic blanket in the living room (or whatever room works best for you). Pack up a basket just like you would for an outdoor picnic and then bring it into the living room. Using a picnic basket adds to the overall mood—and you don't have to worry about the ants! Splurge on some champagne and be sure to pack your champagne glasses. This makes for a cozy and romantic holiday feast.

ROMANTIC IDEAS FOR NEW YEAR'S DAY

Most people probably don't think of New Year's Day as a romantic holiday, but in fact, it can be one of the most rewarding, especially if you think of it as the beginning of a whole new year to spend together with your love. And New Year's Day is usually a quiet day at home—an intimate and perfect setting for romance! This section contains ideas for unique ways to warm your lover's heart on the first day of the year.

Breakfast With the Baby

♥ Wake up your lover on New Year's Day with breakfast in bed, with a twist. Dress up as Baby New Year in a giant diaper. Have a "Happy New Year" sash draped across your chest and wear a bonnet on your head. Hang a pacifier around your neck for effect. You can serve breakfast on baby plates with baby utensils, and orange juice or coffee in a baby bottle. Or you can use New Year's-type utensils and serve orange juice in champagne glasses. And be sure to add a party hat and noisemaker to the tray!

The Calendar of Love

♥ If you want to give your lover something to look forward to for the coming year, give him or her a calendar or daily planner. Carefully choose one that reflects a favorite theme or interest, and then add your own surprises to it. Pick random days throughout the year to write in romantic plans, or simply place heart-shaped stickers on days that you want to set aside for doing something special together. If you're planning a gift of a vacation or attendance at a special event, clip the tickets to the page for the month or week they are to be used in. And make sure to write "I love you!" every so often on days throughout the calendar. Your romantic flair will make a rather ordinary gift quite personal and extraordinary.

Pick A Date

♥ This is a nice variation on the *Calendar of Love* idea (page 109). Do you sit down each January with a calendar for the new year and write in the birthdays of friends and family members? Of all those birthdays, there is only one for each of you. It's a shame that out of the 365 days in a year, there's only one when you wake up expecting special treatment. To overcome this, mark an extra day or two on the calendar specifically for treating your lover like royalty. Mark down days for giving your partner massages, baths, special dinners, and other romantic surprises. Gifts are not necessary; the idea is to designate a day devoted to your lover, a day full of romantic adventures.

A variation on this idea is to sign up for many different dates but with less time-consuming ideas—a back rub here, a movie choice there, a breakfast in bed there. You choose to do whatever you want, whenever you want to do it.

Sharing Your Resolutions

♥ At one time or another, we have all made a New Year's resolution—to cut down on the sweets, exercise twice a week, get involved in community activities, or whatever. Doing this on your own is fine, but doing it together with your mate is an activity that will strengthen your bond of love. For instance, write a list that includes three of each of the following:

❑ Things you want to continue doing.

❑ Things you want to do more of.

❑ Things you want to do less of.

❑ Things you want to do for your mate.

❑ Things you want to do with your mate.

Make two copies of your list. Keep one for yourself and give your partner the other, making sure he or she has read your list. Then, periodically throughout the year, get together to read over your lists again. Give a surprise romantic dinner whenever your partner accomplishes one of his or her goals. You can write the particular resolution on a place card for your lover, as a reminder that his or her personal accomplishments are important to you. This technique can be employed both to open up your minds to dreams and fantasies and to inspire romantic ideas.

Final Romantic Thoughts on New Year's Celebrations

With a whole year behind you and a brand new one ahead, this holiday is the perfect time to look back on your time together, as well as to look toward your future. New Year's celebrations are renowned for fun and romance, so take advantage of the atmosphere surrounding this holiday, and ring in the new year with love.

7. Valentine's Day

T he universal symbol of Valentine's Day is a red heart, and this says just about all you need to know about the meaning of this holiday. Yes, this is the one day of the year that is clearly staked out for expressions of love.

As a day that is the ultimate in romantic tradition, Valentine's Day leads us directly to the objective of this book: to help you inject more romance into your life. In this chapter you will find ideas for gestures of love that are specifically designed for Valentine's Day, but in fact, many of the entries throughout this book have potential on this day. You can adapt and customize many of these ideas for your own individual situation. Have a happy and loving Valentine's Day!

ROMANTIC VALENTINE'S DAY GIFTS

The theme of Valentine's Day is love, and expressing your love in words is a must. It is also fitting to show your love with something more permanent by giving a gift. This section will give you ideas for ways to give a special Valentine that is truly a gift from the heart.

The Personal Touch

♥ Buying a thoughtful gift for your partner is one way to show you care, but to make your Valentine's gift truly romantic, make it a one-of-a-kind offering. This can be accomplished by personalizing any gift you choose to give. The following are ideas for ways to make your gift truly special:

❐ Write a poem or a message on your gift that exemplifies your relationship or expresses your feelings of love. Something written in this way can make your gift much more personal and treasured. Write the message inside a book, on a bottle of wine, or on the back of a painting.

❐ If a gift can fit only a smaller message, then express your thoughts by inscribing a quote, an inside joke, or a short message from the heart on the gift. Or choose a few lines from one of your lover's favorite songs or poems. Any gift that can be enhanced with a message is suitable. Some possibilities include a music box, wristwatch, briefcase, wallet, purse, towel, vase, goblet or champagne glass, belt, book, or robe.

❐ Give a gift that symbolizes your relationship. There is a wide variety of possibilities for this type of gift. Examples include: a globe to symbolize your mutual love of travel; a plant or flower pot to symbolize the growth in your relationship; or candles to symbolize enlightenment. Make your gift a personal and moving tribute.

❐ Give a teddy bear or other stuffed animal and tie a heart-shaped locket around its neck that contains your picture or a picture of the two of you.

Alluring Gift Wrap

♥ Set the tone for a seductive evening by presenting your gift in a sexy fashion. Wrap the gift in a silky nightshirt or other sensual apparel and tie it with lace. Make a card, using a sexy picture of yourself on the front. Write a loving and provocative message on the card, then leave an imprint of your lips on it. Also include a few coupons for massages and intimate activities of your lover's choice in the card. Finally, scent the gift with your characteristic perfume or cologne. This gesture is sure to set your lover's heart on fire.

Out With the Old, In With the New

♥ Most women love getting new lingerie (and most men love seeing them wear it). Use this idea to excite your sweetheart when she looks for her lingerie on Valentine's Day. Prior to Valentine's Day, buy your lover some new lingerie. Replace the old lingerie in her drawer or closet with the new. This is a surprise you won't witness, but you will be sure of its effect when she faces you with her luxurious new undergarments. The smile in her eyes will tell the story. Ladies, you can buy your man silk boxer shorts or other sexy undergarments. You can also use the occasion to buy each other matching bathrobes and towels.

The Classic Romance

♥ For an amusing Valentine's Day gift, make your very own fairy tale. Create your own unique story with accompanying pictures. You can either draw the illustrations yourself or use photographs.

Another way to create a fairy tale is to buy a short children's book that you think is appropriate. Make photocopies of a few photographs of yourself and your lover, and perhaps friends and family members, enlarging them to a number of different sizes (check with a local copy shop for color photocopying services). Then change the names of the characters in the book to your name, your lover's, and your friends' and relatives' names. You can do this by carefully covering the print with a layer of correction fluid (such as Liquid Paper); when it dries, write in the appropriate names. You can also use this technique to change some of the lines in the story to make it more personal. After you finish customizing the written portion, cut out the heads from the photocopies and paste appropriate-sized heads on the bodies of the proper characters in the book. This homage to your relationship is a way to recall something of the magic of your childhood days.

A Puzzle of Love

♥ If your mate has a head for puzzles, this gift idea will be perfect. Buy a child's jigsaw puzzle that has approximately twenty pieces. Have a color copy made of a favorite photograph of the two of you, and paste this onto the front of the puzzle. On the back, write a personalized love message or simply, "I Love You." Once the glue dries, you will be able to cut through the photograph from the opposite side along the lines of the puzzle pieces, using a single-edge razor blade or utility knife. You can cover the top of the puzzle box top with color copy of either the same or a different photograph.

Another way to use a puzzle to show your affection, is to make a personalized crossword or find-a-word puzzle. Use your names, any private jokes you may have, favorite colors and foods, and terms of affection. To make the puzzle durable, you may want to have it laminated.

Either of these gifts will make a wonderful keepsake that can be added to, or simply treasured.

Flicker Fun

♥ Make your own flicker animation drama. To make this witty gift, buy an unlined note pad and draw a simple scene on each page, changing it slightly from page to page so that it resembles a cartoon when you flick the note pad. For instance, you could draw a cartoon of stick figures kissing each other, while little hearts move upward in the air. Title the cartoon, "How I felt during our first kiss." This could be one of those items you may discover years later that reminds you of those silly and impulsive romantic times.

Valentine Cards

♥ Valentine's Day is a time to proclaim your love. Don't just buy a greeting card with a clichéd expression inside and sign your name at the bottom; write something yourself! It doesn't have to be long or earth-shattering verse—the point is that it must come from you and be something personal, something that will have meaning only for the two of you.

The following are simple ideas for a truly personal, meaningful expression:

❐ One idea is to write "I love you" in as many languages as possible. The following is a list of foreign translations:

French	Je t'aime (jeh-TEM)
German	Ich liebe dich (eesh-leebeh-deesh)
Spanish	Te quiero (tay-KEY-ehr-oh)
Italian	Ti-amo (tee-AH-mo)
Portuguese	Amo-te (a-MOO-teh)
Dutch	Ik houser van jou (eek-hooser-von-djou)
Russian	Ya vas liubliu (ya-VAS-lyou-blyou)
Hebrew	Ani ohev otah [man to woman]
	Ani ohev et otha [woman to man]

❐ Make a giant heart or Cupid out of red construction paper. On the card write reasons why you love your mate or reasons why you want your mate to be your Valentine. One clever way to do this is to write your lover's name vertically down the left side of the card and draw a heart around each letter. Then, for each letter, write a phrase about why you love him or her. For example, if your partner's name is Scott, you could write:

S is for your sensitivity
C is for your cute nose
O is for your obliging nature
T is for your thoughtfulness
T is for your tenderness.

❐ Create a fun card using ideas like comics, foldouts, or cutout windows of Valentine characters and scenes. If you need help with illustrations, cut out parts of those inexpensive Valentine's cards designed for kids.

❐ Make a copy of your favorite romantic picture of your mate or of the two of you together, and put this picture on a card with a warm, reflective passage below. Another idea is to write a poem or love letter on the card and use a color copy of the photo as the background. As an added touch, you might dab a little perfume or cologne on the card to stimulate your lover's sense of smell.

❐ Make a card using copies of photographs of you and your partner as kids. Write some funny captions based on what you imagine you might have said to each other as youngsters.

OTHER ROMANTIC VALENTINE'S DAY IDEAS

Valentine's Day is the one day of the year to really go all-out with expressions of affection. In addition to giving your partner a gift, use one or more of the ideas in this section to make your Valentine's Day an all-day celebration of the love you feel for each other.

Romantic Songs

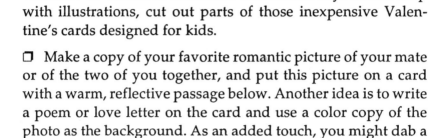 It is truly amazing how hearing an old song can take you back to the exact moment someone gave that song meaning for you. Music can be a very powerful and romantic medium for expressing your affection. One way to let your lover know you are thinking about him or her, and to keep you in his or her thoughts, is to play that special song over the phone. Just call and let the music play, without even saying hello or goodbye. This gesture could make your lover melt.

Here's another musical idea for Valentine's Day. Spend some time prior to Valentine's Day in making a cassette tape of love songs that the two of you hold especially dear. Play the tape during a romantic dinner, place it secretly in the tape deck of your lover's car, or simply give it as a gift. You can also share some romantic time by making a tape of love songs together.

Let Me Count the Ways

♥ No two loving relationships are the same. We all have our own wonderful and distinctive reasons for loving that special someone. The reasons are as diverse and unique as the partners we have chosen to share our lives with. Compile a list of the reasons you love your partner and write it in a letter or on a parchment scroll using a calligraphy marker. Or write each reason on separate little cards, then scatter the cards around the house or apartment for your partner to discover. You might consider embellishing each card with a rosebud, a chocolate kiss, or other romantic touch. Or you can mail the cards one at a time, providing your mate with a heartwarming surprise with each day's mail delivery. This makes a nice stimulant for the holiday of love.

Valentine Surprise

♥ Be sneaky about it! If you can gain access your sweetheart's place without being caught, then decorate the place with a Valentine's theme. First, plant flowers throughout the house or apartment. A single flower and note can be placed on a pillow, dressing mirror, shower head, over personal pictures, or in a lingerie or underwear drawer. You can write cards with riddles, poems, or limericks to lead your love to the hiding places. The gradual flower discoveries will provide little sparks of emotion in your lover's heart. Then fill a special room with red and white balloons and ribbons, Valentine cutouts, banners, and other decorations. You may want to try to enhance the atmosphere by replacing some white light bulbs with red ones or by putting a red cloth over a lamp. (If you do this, make sure the cloth doesn't actually come into contact with the light bulb, so there is no risk of fire.) Take that extra step and utilize

The Story of Valentine's Day

In the days of the Roman Empire, the Emperor Claudius II (also known as Claudius the Cruel), was said to have had a difficult time attracting men to join his army because they did not want to leave their families or sweethearts. The Emperor therefore ordered that no more marriages were to take place and that all engagements were off. A Christian priest named Valentine then began to marry young couples secretly. When Claudius found out about the secret marriages, he ordered the priest sent to prison. Valentine remained in the dungeon until his death, on the 14th of February in the year 270.

Several centuries later, when Christianity was adopted and began to take hold throughout the Roman Empire, the Church sought to do away with pagan holidays that it considered undesirable. One of these was a fertility festival called Lupercalia, which took place in February. As part of this celebration, the names of Roman maidens would be placed in a box, and the young men would each draw one name. Each young man was then supposed to accept the girl drawn as his love for a year or longer. The Church replaced this festival with a tamer, modified version that it called Valentine's Day, in honor of the martyred priest Valentine. As Valentine's Day spread to other countries and as the years went by, this holiday continued to evolve and develop new customs.

the element of surprise to envelop your sweetheart in a romantic ambience.

Valentine Treats

♥ Most of our major holidays have characteristic gifts associated with them. Valentine's Day is particularly known as
a day for giving chocolate. Make sure to include some quality
chocolate as part of your gift. Other treats, like Hershey's
Kisses, Hershey's Hugs, red and white M&M's, cinnamon
hearts, and other heart-shaped candies can be used liberally as
decorations or as part of other gifts. You can also make heart-
shaped desserts in keeping with the Valentine's Day theme.
One idea is to make jumbo heart-shaped cookies with messages
written in icing on the tops.

A Mysterious Valentine

♥ Are you into risk-taking? Try placing an anonymous Valentine's Day card in a place where your lover is likely to
find it, but where anyone might have left it. In the card, you
can describe a hidden passion that you have secretly been
nurturing for a number of years. Leave the message vague
enough so that it might or might not be from you. If you are
secure in your relationship, you can go even further with this
idea. Beginning a few days before Valentine's Day, leave a
couple of cards for your lover in places anyone might have
access to (in the mailbox, under the front door, on your lover's
car windshield). Send your lover flowers—unsigned, of course.
If your lover mentions the cards or the flowers to you, act as if
you know nothing about them. Then, in the last anonymous
card, include an invitation to a meeting in a specified location
at a certain time on Valentine's Day. If your lover mentions the
proposed meeting to you, encourage him or her to go out of
curiosity. When your partner discovers the true identity of his
or her secret lover, romantic sparks are sure to fly!

Food of Love

♥ Make the centerpiece of this day of love a team affair by creating a special, romantic Valentine's dinner. Make this dinner part of a complete Valentine's Day celebration by using it together with some of the other ideas in this chapter. If you have kids, send them to your parents' place or to a babysitter for the night. This is a time for you and your mate alone.

For the dinner itself, try something outside of your normal fare, like fondue, shish kebob, or seafood. For dessert, make heart-shaped cookies, cakes, cupcakes, a gelatin mold, or some other special treat. Remember to think atmosphere! Carry the theme of the meal through all the decor, with lighting, music, a special tablecloth, linen napkins, china, and crystal—break out those dishes you thought you would never use! Use a potpourri warmer, incense, or scented candles to add a romantic fragrance to the air; scents are very powerful in creating memories. And make sure to unplug the telephone! These personal touches will elevate the day beyond the ordinary and make for a truly memorable Valentine's Day.

Your Personal Vintage

♥ If you serve wine with your special dinner, personalize it by using your own label. Some wine stores and mail-order catalogs sell wine with labels made up to say whatever you choose. Or you can simply glue your label over the manufacturer's label on any bottle of wine you buy. To make your label look authentic, use a computer for the lettering, and decorate the label with hearts, flowers, Cupids, and/or a message of love. Have some fun and pretend you are serving your own brand of famous wine from an exotic land.

You can also incorporate this idea into a restaurant celebration and surprise your mate. Give the restaurant your custom-made label ahead of time and have them fasten it to a fine bottle of wine. At dinner, after the waiter pours the first glass, have him set the bottle in the center of the table, then wait for the discovery to be made.

The Tree of Love

♥ Make your own Valentine plant. Buy a small potted plant or tree. Decorate the pot with red paint, paper, or anything else along traditional Valentine lines. Cut out paper hearts and hang them on the branches. For an especially pleasing touch, write different things on the hearts, such as reasons why you love your partner, private jokes, meaningful quotes, a dinner invitation, or sexy messages. Another great idea is to put personal pictures on the hearts. Hang candy on the branches as well. This idea has added meaning because plants represent growth—in this case, the growth of your love.

Building Excitement

♥ When you are falling in love, anything that doesn't have to do with your sweetheart seems tedious, and when you must be away from the object of your affections, everything you see or hear reminds you of your lover. These reminders warm your heart and build your anticipation of your next meeting. When Valentine's Day is approaching, build up the excitement by sending your partner a different flower each day for the seven days prior to the event, and attach a different message to each flower. This is romance of a most pure order. The messages can all be straightforward romantic sentiments, or you may want to give a few clues about your planned agenda for Valentine's Day. If you are planning to take your lover to a play or concert, or for short weekend trip, attach the tickets to the last flower you send.

Another way to build excitement is to hide love letters in various places where your mate will find them throughout the day. Try to word the letters in such a way that they will heighten expectations of the time later in the day when the two of you will finally see each other.

Love Set Sail

♥ This idea is filled with symbolism relating to love and the sharing of two lives. Have you ever put a message in a bottle and set it free on the water? Use this as an idea for a loving gesture. Take a special memento of your relationship and place it in a miniature boat or glass bottle to be set free in a large body of water. The memento should be something that the two of you hold dear: a love letter or a short story one of you has written about your lives, a special gift you shared, or perhaps a poem. Get together to bestow some parting wishes on the boat or bottle, then set it free. This little vessel's journey is one that will parallel your romantic journey. You are sending out a time capsule of your love. Watch it as long as you possibly can and think about your good fortune in sharing your life with this special person at your side. Trés romantique!

Touch Your Lover With Song

♥ If you have musical abilities, this is a special project for you. The idea here is to write a personal and romantic song and present it in an amorous way. You can perform it in front of a fireplace or in a room warmed with candles and incense. If you are on vacation or live in a warm climate, then you can present it at the beach or on a boat, an intimate and emotional setting for your performance. The possibilities for special touches are endless. To provide an audio memoir, you can record your special song on a cassette, then give your lover both a copy of the lyrics and the recording for a keepsake. If you are more gifted with words than with music, this idea can work with a poem written to your beloved and read out loud with the feeling that only the poet can provide.

Final Romantic Thoughts on Valentine's Day

Even though you are expected to be romantic on Valentine's Day, you can still "wow" your lover by making a little extra effort and doing something completely unexpected. Think about what you would normally do for your lover on this day; then ask yourself what you can do to make this Valentine's Day a shade more romantic. With a whole holiday dedicated to romance, your amorous ideas are as sure to hit the mark as Cupid's arrow.

In the Name of Love

Many famous works of art and music throughout history were inspired by romance. Some were created as gifts, others to impress a special someone.

The French composer Louis-Hector Berlioz was inspired to write his famous "Symphonie Fantastique" by the love of a woman. However, this woman left Berlioz while he was only halfway through the symphony. Her rejection so infuriated the composer, that the tone of the third and fourth movements of this piece was changed entirely. The third movement, "March to the Scaffold," and the fourth movement, "Night of the Witches Sabbath," were so impressive that Berlioz's love returned to marry him.

One of the great architectural works of our world, the famous Taj Mahal, was built by the Mogul ruler Shah Jahan in loving memory of his wife, Mumtaz Mahal, who died in childbirth in 1631. Today, over 300 years later, her memory has been kept alive by her husband's grand romantic gesture.

8. *Other Holidays*

We feel that every day is a good day for romance, but holidays give you an added excuse to shower your loved one with attention. Now that we have given you ideas for the major occasions throughout the year, we would like to show you how romantic other holidays can be.

Holidays like Mother's Day, Father's Day, Independence Day, and Halloween are not normally considered especially romantic. But this can actually work to your advantage. Because you are not expected to do anything romantic on these holidays, your efforts will be that much more appreciated.

The basic idea behind romance is to enjoy the time spent with your partner—have fun! You can do something new and spontaneous, or you can do something you have done many times before, just as long as your effort carries the message that you care.

ROMANTIC IDEAS FOR MOTHER'S DAY
AND FATHER'S DAY

Mother's Day and Father's Day are holidays that you may not
think of as being romantic, but what more perfect occasion is there
for you to honor your spouse? Although you may have always
considered these holidays as times to celebrate your mother or
father, they also offer wonderful opportunities for you to tell how
much you respect, love, and appreciate your mate.

Breakfast in Bed

♥ Although this idea has been around for many years, it is
still one of the most appreciated, and rarely fails to please.
Wake your mate up—before the children do—with his or her
favorite breakfast fare. Make sure to include on the tray the
morning paper, a flower, and a card. Turn on some relaxing
music, and let your mate enjoy breakfast without the hustle and
bustle of a normal morning.

If you can't beat the children to it, let them help you. Set the
tray up with the morning paper, a flower, and any cards and
gifts from the kids. Supervise the breakfast preparations, and
then make sure that your partner gets to spend the morning in
whatever way he or she likes best, whether that means taking
a walk in park with the family or spending some quiet time
alone to relax and read the Sunday paper.

Family Fun

♥ The best part of being a parent is enjoying your children.
Kids remind us of the energy, enthusiasm, and spontaneity
that help enhance any relationship. On holidays for honoring
parents, let your children lead the way. Spend the day outdoors
with your partner and kids, and just enjoy their company. Take
your family to a park, botanical garden, or beach, or simply into
the backyard. Allow yourselves time to play together. This will
strengthen your bond of love.

The Dinner Date

♥ Get together with your children to honor your mate with romance. If your children are at the age where they enjoy playing make-believe, take advantage of this. Instead of taking your partner out to dinner, stay home and prepare dinner with the kids. In the morning, give your partner an invitation to dress for dinner and to meet you in the dining room at a specific time. Feed the children their dinner early, then let them help you set the table with the "good" linens and china and prepare dinner. Next, dress the children in dark pants or skirts, white shirts, and bow ties, and let them pretend to be your waiters or waitresses for the evening. After the evening is over, let the children line up and take a bow. This idea is endearing to almost any parent, and lets you have a special dinner with your mate.

Finishing Touches

♥ Don't forget the details on your partner's special day. These are just a few little items that show your partner how thoughtful you are:

❏ Send flowers or balloons to your mate with a card attached letting him or her know of your love and admiration.

❏ Leave a flower on your mate's pillow at the end of the day.

❏ Have a bottle of wine and a rented movie ready to enjoy with your partner after the children are asleep. And don't forget the candlelight!

❏ Leave a new pair of silk pajamas for your husband or a new silk nightgown for your wife, to be found at bedtime.

❏ Leave a love letter on your partner's pillow. Wrap it in a lace ribbon, or leave it with his or her favorite candy.

ROMANTIC IDEAS FOR THE FOURTH OF JULY

What a perfect day for some romantic fireworks! Although this day is a celebration of our country's independence, the festivities for this holiday are also just right for romance. Learn to take advantage of every opportunity to let your mate know how much you care.

Flag Fun

♥ As an amorous surprise, wait in a dark room, wrapped only in a large American flag—or strategically placed smaller flags—with sparklers or other patriotic paraphernalia around you. Decorate the room all in red, white, and blue if you can. Turn on some patriotic music, perhaps even "The Star-Spangled Banner," and then call your mate in. This makes for a very patriotic and romantic greeting.

Dependence Day

♥ Make your lover a Fourth of July dinner, perhaps a barbecue for two, to be served in colonial-style clothing. Use sparklers instead of candles for a more festive feeling, and then present your loved one with your personal "Declaration of Complete and Utter Dependence" written on a parchment scroll. To take this a step further, try to word your declaration in a fashion similar to that of the real Declaration of Independence.

Taking It All In

♥ The Fourth of July is full of celebrations and events that become romantic opportunities when you do them together. Look in your local newspaper for listings of Independence Day activities. Some ideas include the following:

❐ Go to an outdoor concert at night with a blanket and some refreshments and cuddle up under the stars.

❐ Find a quiet spot on the beach to build a fire and watch fireworks.

❐ If you live in an apartment, go up to the roof of your building to watch fireworks.

❐ Camp out under the stars.

❐ Temporarily "sneak away" from a family function to watch the fireworks alone together.

❐ Take a boat out on a bay or lake for a late dinner and a spectacular view of fireworks displays.

❐ Have a barbecue or picnic for two in a nearby park.

Whatever your choice of celebrations, it can be truly romantic if you do it together.

ROMANTIC IDEAS FOR HALLOWEEN

Halloween may seem like a strange time to be thinking about romance, but it doesn't have to be. Try the ideas that follow and you'll see how you can translate ghosts and ghouls into hearts and flowers.

Late Night Frights

♥ Sometimes Hollywood provides practical ideas for those of us in search of romance. After the Halloween party is over and you have met all of the neighborhood trick-or-treaters, enter your own Gothic world through movies. Make sure the room is dark and spooky, light a jack-o'-lantern, and watch a good horror movie or two. There are usually scary movies on television on Halloween night, but you can also rent a video if there is a particular film you want to see. Some good suggestions include: *Halloween, The Exorcist, Carrie, The Haunting, Psycho, The Changeling, Night of the Living Dead, Spirits of the Dead, Nightmare on Elm Street, The Black Cat, Frankenstein,* and *Carnival of Souls.* A scary movie is sure to have the two of you reaching for each other. You won't want to be sleeping alone on a night like this!

Jack-O'-Lanterns

♥ Carving a pumpkin for Halloween can be a great activity for bringing you closer to your loved one. Go pumpkin-picking on a weekend afternoon and find the perfect pumpkin. You can each get your own, or you can get one or more for the two of you. When you get the pumpkin home, spread out some newspaper and dig in. First, cut a hole in the top of your pumpkin, and remove the seeds inside. Then draw a face on the pumpkin. Make it as silly or as scary as you like. Next, take a sharp knife and start cutting along your design. When you're finished, insert a candle in the bottom of the pumpkin and light it. If each of you has your own pumpkin, you can have fun with this by having a carving contest, or by having each of you try to make your pumpkin look like the other person. This is prime time for sharing childhood Halloween stories.

You can set up different jack-o'-lanterns all over your house and then turn off all the lights for a spooky but romantic effect.

Altered Identities

♥ Would you like to lose yourself in another identity? Then Halloween is just the excuse you've been looking for. Make or rent costumes for you and your mate to wear to your own private costume party. For a romantic twist, dress up as a romantic couple from literature, the movies, or history. Some fun suggestions include:

❑ Mark Antony and Cleopatra.

❑ Odysseus and Penelope.

❑ Romeo and Juliet.

❑ King Henry VIII and Anne Boleyn (try not to lose your head!).

❑ Morticia and Gomez Addams.

❑ Rhett Butler and Scarlett O'Hara.

❑ Frankenstein and his bride.

Stay in character throughout the night to make Halloween just a little more interesting.

Fulfill A Fantasy

♥ Does your partner have a character fantasy that he or she has always wanted to fulfill? Halloween is the perfect time to make your lover's fantasy come true. If she has always loved *Gone With the Wind,* or if he has always wanted a date with Marilyn Monroe, now is your chance to take your partner's breath away.

Rent or make a costume for the appropriate character and try to be that person for your lover for the whole night. No matter how goofy you may feel, keep in character and it will add to the romance. Use appropriate props to carry the theme through the night. You may want to act out a scene for your partner, ad-libbing your lines to fit the situation.

To carry the fantasy one step further, you can also rent or make a costume for your partner to wear. When your lover comes home on Halloween, you can already be in costume and ask him or her (in character, of course) to change into costume.

No matter which way you choose to fulfill the fantasy, the thought and effort should knock your lover over. You can take it from there.

The Trail

♥ Use a little mystery to lead your lover straight into your arms. Leave a trail of notes and Halloween items for your partner to find when he or she gets home. Start with a note attached to a bag of Halloween candy that sends your mate to the kitchen to find yet another note. Word these notes so that your mate collects a different item—like a corkscrew, wine glasses (with fake spiders in them), a bottle of wine—at each stop. If you are feeling particularly amorous, instruct your lover to remove an article of clothing at each stop, and leave a trail of your own clothing between the notes. The last note should send your mate to the bedroom door, which will have a sign on it that says, "trick or treat?" Wait inside the bedroom, either in costume or barely dressed in black. Our guess is that your lover will pick the treat!

A Gothic Dinner

♥ Here is a lesson on how to set a specific mood. You want to create a Halloween theme for a romantic dinner with your partner, so use everything you have available. Black taper candles or a jack-o'-lantern is perfect for eerie lighting. Buy a tape with the sounds of a haunted house or perhaps some Gothic-type organ music to use for your "background music." Use a black or orange tablecloth, with orange or black flowers at your place settings. For a romantic, seasonal touch for your table setting, bring in a basket of brightly colored fall leaves. You can hang fake spider webs in the corners and doorways to add to the spooky mood.

Leave your mate an invitation that morning, with a small bag of Halloween candy, specifying whether your want him or her to arrive in costume or in black formal wear. Whatever you choose, stick with your eerie theme. If you opt for costumes, make sure yours is mysterious. After all, Little Bo Peep would hardly be hanging spider webs in her kitchen! If you go for black attire, stick to your best clothes, like your slinkiest little black dress, or a black shirt and slacks, or perhaps even a tuxedo. Now that you have set your mood, have a little ghostly fun!

Final Romantic Thoughts on Other Holidays

By putting on your thinking cap to come up with romantic ideas for holidays that aren't usually considered romantic, you are teaching yourself how to be creative. You can make any holiday more romantic with just a little thought, and you and your lover get to reap the rewards. So remember, just because the card stores haven't caught on to the possibility of romance on these days, that doesn't mean you can't.

Part II

Creating Very Special Moments

In Part I, we focused on romantic things to do for your partner on holidays, birthdays, and other personal days. Of course, you shouldn't have to wait until Valentine's Day or a birthday to make a romantic gesture. It is just as loving (and important) to create special moments during the routine of your daily lives. Variety is the key to keeping a fresh perspective on romance.

Part II offers ideas that will help you to create such special moments during the everyday hustle and bustle of life—moments in which the focus is on you and your lover, and the two of you are free to explore your own special romantic universe.

Romantic moments are what really define your love relationship. That is why it is so important to leave the workday behind and allow yourself time to dream. Dreaming allows you to be alone in your mind with your lover, and it helps to encourage creative romantic ideas, both of which help to establish or strengthen a passionate bond between you. People who are romantic are invariably passionate, not just about their partners, but about most aspects of their lives. Passionate people feel vibrant and alive.

Love is present in your day-to-day lives, but romance is felt in those precious moments when you and your lover take priority over everything else. Just look to the big screen for verification of this. Hollywood specializes in romantic moments. Just about every movie, whether it is an action film, comedy, or drama, has some love interest. Screenwriters illustrate how romance can flourish in any situation through the following simple equation: man, plus woman, plus time alone together, equals romance. *One of the single most useful romantic actions often is simply creating time to be alone with your partner.* The special moments often follow naturally.

Never take your partner for granted. Each day, look at your lover as if you are seeing him or her for the first time. Try to relive the thrill you felt each time you looked at your partner when you began falling in love. Remembering the smallest details when thinking of or talking to your lover will keep the romance fresh and alive. When the two of you try something new, be liberal with compliments.

Mark Twain once said that he could live for two months on a good compliment.

Try to maintain an awareness of the romance between you and your lover, no matter how long you have been together. And remember, it doesn't matter where or when you try to create romantic moments; the importance lies in your effort.

9. *Surprises*

*T*hink back to the best times of your life. Were many of these special moments planned, or did they occur when you expected nothing out of the ordinary? In other words, did these times include the element of surprise? Most likely they did. These occasions stand out in your memory precisely because they were out of the ordinary, as well as unexpected. They are the moments that are fondly recalled throughout your life—one-time occurrences that cannot be duplicated.

Year in and year out, certain days like birthdays, Christmas, and Valentine's Day are special in their own right, but you can create a whole new category of loving gestures when you take an ordinary day and turn it into a holiday of its own, a celebration of your love. We don't deny that there are day-to-day difficulties that may distract your romantic efforts; however, we do suggest you attempt to climb over these daily barriers from time to time with a romantic surprise for your partner.

Surprising your lover for no reason at all is one of the best ways of showing that he or she is on your mind. With a little effort, you can create wonderful moments that generate deep feelings of intimacy.

When planning a surprise, make sure your partner's calendar is clear for the time you need. (You wouldn't want to prepare a surprise romantic dinner, then later discover that he or she has an after-work dentist appointment or a company meeting.)

Try to be sensitive to your partner's moods. Paying close attention will help you figure out the best time to surprise your lover with a little romance. For instance, if your lover hasn't had a break from the pressures of his or her job in a while, or if he or she has been feeling down in the doldrums, a romantic interlude can provide welcome relief. This little extra attention shows your partner how much he or she means to you. Read through the following ideas. Maybe one (or more than one) will be just right for you.

Early Morning Surprise

♥ Breakfast in bed is one of the more traditional ways of doing something special. And you don't have to wait for a special occasion to do this; any ordinary day will do. Of course, be sure to include your partner's favorite breakfast fare, along with a copy of the morning paper, and perhaps a cup of aromatic gourmet coffee. As an added touch, put on your partner's regular morning radio station while he or she is enjoying breakfast. For special occasions, you might toast the morning together with sparkling mimosas (champagne and orange juice cocktails).

Serving your lover breakfast in bed, no matter how simple or elaborate, is one surprise that never fails to please, no matter how often you do it.

Helping Hands

♥ Think of how nice it would make your lover feel to come home to find his or her housework and errands already done. Your surprise can be anything: washing the car; cleaning the pool; doing the laundry; mopping the kitchen floor; taking the kids to their after-school activities; preparing your lover's lunch; mowing the lawn; or any other dreaded chore. Such giving and consideration will be noticed and appreciated. It reassures your partner of your support and understanding.

An Impulsive Bouquet of Love

♥ If you and your loved one are out for a walk in the woods or a park, keep your eyes open. If you happen to spot some wildflowers, dash over and pick a natural bouquet. Present them to your sweetheart with romantic ceremony. Be kind and choose only flowers growing in abundance (and be aware of park fines).

Noontime Messages

♥ If your partner brings his or her lunch to work, sneak a romantic note in with it. This small, delightful surprise will make your lover smile all day. This is also a good way to keep your thoughts paired even when the two of you are physically apart.

Spreading the News

♥ Take advantage of the element of surprise to knock your mate's socks off. If you have an important announcement to make—a promotion, a new job, a pregnancy, an upcoming vacation—reveal your good news through surprise. Try one of the following tactics:

❏ Write your news on an index card, then place the card in your mate's cereal box.

❏ Tape your message on an audiocassette tape. Have it set and ready to play in the tape deck of your lover's car.

❏ Announce your news by writing it on a card. Hide the card in your partner's purse or briefcase.

❑ Plant your message in a fortune cookie.

❑ Have a singer (at a bar or restaurant) announce your news.

❑ Write out your news, then tape it to a page in your partner's favorite section of the newspaper.

In order to get the greatest reaction, make your announcement as much of a surprise as possible. Marking such important moments with the element of surprise will keep the memory of them clear over the years.

A Private Performance

♥ Use your hidden talents to conduct a private show exclusively for your partner. Here are three ideas for displaying intimacy through song and poetry.

❑ Memorize a poem that expresses your love. While you are making love, or at another more appropriate time, passionately recite the words to this piece.

❑ Sing a love song to your lover at just the right private moment.

❑ The next time you and your partner are slow dancing to a song whose words express your feelings, quietly sing the words into your lover's ear. You can enhance this sexy, romantic gesture with gentle nudges and soft kisses to your partner's neck and ear.

A Flair for Drama

♥ Create a puppet show that is intensely personal and features you and your mate. There are numerous possibilities here for creativity. (Consider this elaborate idea only if you have a lot of time on your hands.)

For your script, either take a classical story of romance and revise it to reflect the story of you and your lover, or write an original story. Even if you lack a flair for writing, you can make up for it through costumes and set design. A simple story of your meeting and the development of your love can be the basis for an artistic spectacle to knock your lover over. This is a super idea for a special occasion.

The Melody of Your Song

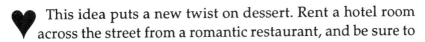 Did you ever notice that many movies have romantic scenes that take place in a piano bar? Take this tried-and-true setting and give it a romantic twist of your own. Instead of simply requesting the pianist to sing "your song" to your sweetheart, make it an even sweeter surprise by joining in the song yourself, or by singing the song alone. This gesture is sure to touch your lover's heart.

Surprise at the Mall

When out shopping together, pretend to have an errand to run, or perhaps a phone call to make. Arrange to meet later at a designated place and time. Show up with a handful of goodies—a card, flowers, chocolates, and/or balloons. The spontaneity factor here is a sure winner.

Or, while you are shopping, take notice of something your partner likes but doesn't buy (maybe because the item is too pricey, or because he or she isn't in a "buying" mood). Again, pretend to have an errand to take care of, and arrange to meet later at a designated place and time. This time, show up with that item all wrapped up with a card on top. Think of the look on your lover's face when you present her with that bracelet she so desired, or that book he really wanted. This little observation and thoughtful gesture is sure to make your lover's day.

Dinner Surprise

This idea puts a new twist on dessert. Rent a hotel room across the street from a romantic restaurant, and be sure to get two keys. Send your lover an invitation at work to meet you at the restaurant for a romantic dinner. The surprise of the dinner invitation alone should please your lover very much. Right after the dinner plates are cleared away, and before the dessert menu comes, pretend to go to the restroom. Instead, give one of the room keys to the waiter, along with instructions to deliver the key to your mate a few minutes after you leave. Then pay the bill, and go to the hotel room. When your mate arrives, greet him or her with dessert and champagne as an ending to your romantic dinner (and the beginning to a romantic night).

A Secret Admirer

♥ Put a little mystery into your relationship. Send flowers or a card to your lover anonymously. Ask someone else to write out the card for you in his or her writing, so that you are not a suspect. When asked if you are the one who has sent the mysterious offering, play innocent to keep your lover in suspense. You can give in after one try, or you can send two or three gifts before disclosing your identity. You can even leave hints in each successive card as to who you are. A little mysterious, but a lot of fun!

Sparks of Passion

♥ Nothing inspires passion and emotion like an unexpected romantic interlude. This first suggestion, which is geared toward females, is a real "fire-starter." Put on some sexy lingerie under your everyday clothing and, if you have long hair, pin it up. When the moment is right, and your partner least expects it, put on some seductive music and turn down the lights. Casually walk up to him, let your hair down, and slowly, sensuously peel off your clothing and show him what you have been hiding.

Here's an idea for the males. Surprise your partner by leaving her a new piece of lingerie in place of her robe while she is in the shower. While you are waiting for her, slip on a pair of silk boxers, turn off the lights, and flood the room with candlelight. As an added surprise, have a bottle of chilled champagne on hand, and perhaps some juicy chocolate-dipped strawberries.

If you are at a party or other type of public gathering, and you want to set a few sparks flying in your lover's imagination, whisper something suggestive and intimate into his or her ear; something that will heighten the anticipation of your next romantic encounter. Perhaps you can tell him that you are wearing a piece of his favorite lingerie under your outfit (or maybe nothing at all). Or you can whisper a romantic reason why you can't wait to be alone with him or her, and are counting the minutes until your next intimate encounter. These little suggestive innuendoes are sure-fire passion starters.

A Surprise at Day's End

♥ At the end of the workday, do you head to your car in a comatose fashion like most people do? Is your ride home so routine that you are barely aware of even making the drive? Wouldn't it be nice to have this routine broken up by something extraordinary?

❑ On an ordinary day, go to your lover's place of employment and decorate his or her car. Use streamers and balloons that bear a variety of messages. To shake up your partner's ride home, make a cassette tape with some very private and personal messages, maybe something that indicates what is waiting for him or her at home. Leave the tape in the tape deck with a little note that says "Play Me." Surely, the drive home will be sparked with anticipation.

❑ For something more traditional, decorate your partner's car with roses and romantic notes, or fill the car with balloons. Have a cassette tape of favorite love songs in the tape deck with a note attached that says "Play Me."

❑ Another idea to break up the monotony of your partner's ride home from work is to provide him or her with a trail of romantic messages. Cut heart-shaped signs from plywood or use "For Sale" signs that have been covered with paper. Write out a romantic message, putting parts of the message on each sign. Line your partner's route home from work with the signs spaced periodically. A little bizarre, maybe, but this idea is sure to surprise your lover at the end of a long workday!

Surprise Messages

♥ The beginning of a romantic relationship is often filled with little surprise intimate messages. Re-create that passion by dropping a small, unexpected message to your lover during the course of his or her day.

☐ Write a romantic message with water-based markers on the bathroom mirror in the morning. It's a great way to start your lover's day.

☐ Sneak into the bathroom while your partner is in the shower and write a spontaneous "I Love You" in the mist on the mirror.

☐ Slip a message into your partner's makeup case that mentions how beautiful she is to you without the makeup.

☐ Write a romantic message across a banner, then hang it in a doorway or across the front of the house.

☐ On a cold winter's day, write a "welcome home" message on a frosty window or door. This should put a smile on your mate's face, especially if he or she has had a bad day.

A Surprise Visit at Work

♥ An unexpected visit to your partner's place of work is always a nice gesture. If the workplace is near a park, pack a lunch, bring a blanket, and enjoy a private midday picnic together. If popping in during the day is not possible, surprise your partner by showing up at the end of the workday. Treat him or her to an unexpected dinner.

Take a Lunch Break

♥ Call your lover at work and ask him or her to meet you for a romantic picnic lunch. Plan to get together somewhere outdoors like an arboretum, a beach, or a park. The simple act of taking time out from your hectic day to relax together will bring pleasure to you both.

Thoughtful Tokens

♥ For no reason at all, occasionally present your lover with thoughtful little tokens. These items can include anything—a pint of your partner's favorite ice cream, a bar of his or her favorite candy, or a bottle of his or her favorite wine. Whatever your partner likes can be included in this special yet simple gesture of your thoughtfulness. If your partner plays tennis, you might bring him or her a new can of tennis balls; or if movies are a passion, present him or her with a favorite video classic. The idea here is to show your partner that you are always thinking of him or her.

Time Out

♥ Making time for each other is a basic element for romance. Occasionally taking time out from one of your favorite personal activities to spend time with your lover will send an impressive message. Surprise your partner with a romantic dinner or lunch during the time you usually sit in front of the television and watch endless hours of a sports program. Or treat your lover to an afternoon at the movies during the time you normally work out at the gym. Put off that afternoon of gardening to go for a peaceful walk with your partner.

Want to approach this idea from a different angle? Make an effort to learn a little about one of your partner's interests (even if it is something you really don't care for). Imagine how surprised and pleased your lover will be when you join in the activity he or she enjoys. This act shows your mate that you respect his or her interests, that you care, and that you are open to new interests.

The Calendar of Love

♥ Buy a monthly wall calendar featuring an appropriate theme for your partner (racecars, dogs, flowers), then fill in some of the days with planned surprises. Pick one day in each month and pencil in "Night Out." If you have purchased tickets to a sports event or a play, tape the tickets to the appropriate date. Write in any other plans you may have in the proper dates. This idea carries even more surprise when the calendar is given at the beginning of the year. This is because, for instance, your mate may not realize until July that there are vacation or show tickets attached somewhere in August. However, you can use this idea at any time of the year.

A Treasure Hunt

♥ Most children dream of coming across a map for buried treasure. Steal this basic idea from childhood to set up a romantic adventure. If you and your partner have made plans to spend time on a beach or at a campsite, this idea is perfect. After buying or making a present for your lover, go to that place and bury the gift. Then walk through the area and map out the trail. Instead of an "X" marking the spot where your gift is buried, use a big red heart. Later on, hand over the "treasure map" to your partner, and watch the adventure begin.

A Trip Down Memory Lane

♥ Put together a scrapbook of memories from your lover's life that focuses on your time together. You might include ticket stubs, theater programs, photos, toys, awards, trophies, newspaper clippings, "remember when" notes, love letters, or florist cards from special occasions. (Always make sure to save these precious "scraps.") If you are really ambitious, you could enlist the help of friends or family and act out some special event in your partner's life on videotape.

This idea may be extensive enough to use as a birthday or anniversary present. Or you can make it a simple, unexpected surprise for no apparent reason.

The Limousine Escort

♥ After you have shared an ordinary breakfast together, surprise your lover with a limousine to escort him or her to work. Don't do anything out of the ordinary during the day, but as your lover leaves the office, greet him or her with the same limousine—with you inside. Put on some romantic music, and open a bottle of wine to propose a toast. After a cruise through the city, have the driver take you to a fine restaurant for a romantic dinner. Afterward, have the limousine driver take you to an quiet, intimate place for a nightcap to end your wonderfully romantic evening.

Friday Suspense

♥ Plan a surprise weekend getaway with your lover, perhaps to a nearby resort or hotel. On the Friday you will be leaving, give your partner little hints and clues that alert him or her to your mysterious weekend plans. Have the first note waiting on the breakfast table. Without mentioning where you're going, this note should alert your partner to fact that you have a special weekend planned. Throughout the day, send a few more messages to your partner at work. These messages, which can be sent by fax or phone, should reveal a bit more information about the weekend—just enough to pique your partner's curiosity. By the time your lover gets home, have a suitcase packed and a taxi waiting to whisk you off to the hotel or the airport, where you will embark on a marvelous weekend getaway.

Starry-Eyed Wishes

♥ How would you like to have a star named after you? Naming a star after your partner is a wonderful way of surprising him or her, and showing just how much you care. You can easily register a star in your lover's name through the International Star Registry. The presentation of this gift can be intimate and definitely romantic.

On a clear night, suggest a romantic walk in the moonlight. Point out some of the constellations, then casually point to the one that includes your partner's star. When your lover looks at you in confusion, hand over the registration papers, and explain that no star could shine as brightly as your love for him or her, but this was the closest you could come.

This is an original and thoughtful gift that shows how much your lover means to you. (For further information, contact the International Star Registry at 1–800–282–3333.)

Reach Out and Touch Someone

♥ When you can't be with your lover, use the telephone to express your love. Put in a call to your partner. When he or she answers the phone, say nothing. Simply play a tape of his or her favorite love song over the phone, then hang up when the song is over. Your lover will know where the call came from.

The same idea can be used by reading your partner's favorite romantic poem. Either tape your personal reading on cassette or do it live. Whichever you decide, keep it emotional and don't allow any lulls in the reading.

Race of Love

♥ If your partner has always fantasized about driving a particular car, rent one for a day (be sure to do this on your partner's day off). Park the car in the driveway before your lover wakes up, and leave the keys on the breakfast table with a note that reads, "Meet me outside." After his or her initial shock, hop into the passenger seat with a picnic basket filled with goodies, and take off for a fabulous day.

Cracker Jack Surprise

♥ Turn one of the rooms in your house into a romantic version of a Cracker Jacks box. You will need lots of balloons (as many as it takes to fill a particular room), a trusted accomplice, a box of Cracker Jacks, and a small gift. Inflate the balloons and put them in large plastic bags. Bring your accomplice these bags, along with the gift, the Cracker Jacks, and a spare house key. While you and your partner are out, have your accomplice go into your home, hide the gift in the chosen room, empty all of the balloons into the room, and close the door. Have your accomplice tape the Cracker Jacks box to the door. On the box, attach a note that reads, "Have fun finding the prize!"

Hiding Spots

♥ One way to have fun with your partner is to hide a gift, then give him or her clues on where to look. If your gift is small, like perfume or a piece of jewelry, you'll find that you can hide it in just about anything. Here are a few ideas:

❑ Buy a new outfit for your partner, pin a dinner invitation to it, then bring the outfit to the dry cleaner's. Have the clerk simply wrap the outfit in plastic and write up a "phony" receipt for it. Later on, ask your partner to please pick up the dry cleaning for you. What a nice surprise will greet your lover when he or she is handed the new outfit, complete with dinner invitation!

❑ Hide a small gift for your partner in some foliage somewhere near your home. Take your partner for a walk, then pretend to spot something in the area where you have hidden the gift. Urge your partner to inspect the area with you. Wait for the look of surprise when your lover discovers a box with his or her name on it.

❏ Freeze a small gift in an ice cube. Later on, use the ice cube in your partner's drink. Heighten the surprise by making the drink a frothy tropical extravaganza that is festively garnished with pieces of fruit, and decorated with paper parasols. This type of drink will momentarily draw attention away from the ice cube.

❏ Place your gift inside a gingerbread house and present it to your partner as though the house is the actual gift. Your partner won't realize that there is more to your gift until the house is half eaten.

❏ Place a small gift inside a balloon. Inflate this balloon, then tie it in with a bouquet of regular balloons. Tape a pin to the gift card as a hint that the balloons should be popped.

Final Romantic Thoughts on Surprises

One of the nicest ways to express feelings of love and appreciation for your partner is to take an ordinary moment and somehow make it special. Surprise loving gestures, no matter how small, serve as sincere messages of your heartfelt feelings. Your partner will appreciate and always remember your special efforts.

10. Creative Dinners

G enerally, most couples eat together. Eating is one activity that everyone has to make time for, and that, at least once a day, is usually shared with a partner.

During the beginning stage of a romantic relationship, going out to dinner is often a special event—time spent alone with your partner. Over time, however, eating together tends to lose its romantic flair and becomes an uneventful part of your daily routine. Why not take this time that has already been set aside and use it to your romantic advantage? In addition to being a perfect time to talk to each other, mealtime can also be the perfect time for romance. To make dinnertime "special," focus on making it more than a humdrum affair.

Of course, the routine of your daily life may be quite hectic, but every once in a while, make an effort to enjoy a romantic dinner with your partner. Just being alone without distractions can do wonders to set the right mood. So arrange to have someone watch the kids, take the phone off the hook, and turn off the television. Even if the meal itself is nothing out of the ordinary, make a habit of lessening outside distractions; it makes it easier to talk to and focus on one another.

Sharing new experiences is a common benefit of being involved in a romantic relationship. Mealtime is the perfect time to do some experimenting. You can prepare a new entrée or dessert, or you can toast your meal together with a new wine.

This chapter offers creative, romantic ideas for everyday meals, as well as more elaborate dinner presentations. Eat and enjoy!

Back in Time

♥ Take a scene or setting from one of your favorite books and try to re-create it for a dinner theme. For example, if you have always been enamored with the historical setting of a Jane Austen or Charlotte Brontë novel, transform your home to reflect this period. You can have the dinner catered, and have servants serve your multiple-course feast. After dessert and coffee, adjourn to the sitting room, where you might entertain your partner with music or a poetry reading. This can be followed with a private ball and dancing all evening long.

A Catered Affair

♥ You don't have to wait for a special occasion to surprise your partner with a catered dinner. Freeing yourselves of ordinary domestic tasks can give you the time you need to think up more romantic schemes. Many catering services are designed to provide meals for small, private affairs. They are listed in your local yellow pages under "Caterers."

A Team Dinner

♥ Making a dinner special doesn't always have to include surprises and decorations. You and your lover can make a dinner unique by preparing it together as a team. You can do this spontaneously with foods you have on hand, or you can make the dinner a more planned affair. Perhaps you would like to make an unusual dish that you have never tried before. With a list of ingredients in hand, make the trip to the local market together. Maybe you can purchase something unique to add to your dinner fare, like some imported cheese or an exotic fruit that is out of season. If the main course you have planned is not too complicated, you might also try your hand at preparing a fancy dessert. The important thing here is that you do everything together.

And remember to have fun with this team effort. The two of you can pretend you are French chefs in a fancy restaurant. Pots and pans everywhere! Make it a fun-filled affair that is a night in itself. Complement your wonderful meal with a favorite wine. Special touches will create long-lasting memories and inspire future team dinners.

Theme Dinner

It is always fun to prepare a theme dinner. Plan a meal that reflects a place or a well-known time period. Hawaiian, Mexican, French, Arabian, or Italian dinner themes are common. Time periods such as the Middle Ages, the Roaring Twenties, and the Fifties are other fun themes. Rent or make appropriate costumes. As an added touch, decorate your home with theme-related items. For example, if you have chosen a Hawaiian theme, you might cut some palm trees out of cardboard and place them throughout the dining room. If you have chosen to center your dinner around the Fifties, put a "homemade" jukebox in the corner of the room, and maybe hang some giant cardboard records from the ceiling.

Be sure to play music that reflects the theme of the evening. Play the part of characters from this era throughout dinner. This idea, which is a lot of fun, also works well for dinner parties with other couples.

A Country-Style Dinner

Want an idea for a fun theme dinner? Buy a couple of bales of hay and pile them in your backyard or living room (if you don't mind vacuuming after). Then plan a romantic country-style dinner either inside or outside. You can serve barbecued chicken, corn on the cob, crisp salad, and fresh bread. Wear overalls and straw hats, and for added mood, go barefoot and chew on a piece of straw. For decorations, hang some outdoor lights, put up a scarecrow, and lean some corn stalks in a corner. On the table, use a gingham tablecloth.

After dinner, let the dancing begin. Have fun square dancing to some fast-paced fiddle music, which you can rent from your local library. When the dancing is over and you are ready to settle down, end the night with some frolicking in the haystack.

Fast Food Romance

♥ In the name of fun, inject a little romance into a take-out dinner. Arrange to have your partner meet you in a picturesque park in the early evening. Tell him or her to wait for you at a specific bench or table. Sneak up behind your lover and surprise him or her with a bag filled with Chinese food. Spread out a blanket and enjoy this special dinner together in an inspired new manner. Between kisses, try feeding each other with chopsticks for an increased feeling of intimacy.

If you and your partner are having dinner in a fast food restaurant, place a small vase of flowers and a lit candle in the middle of the table. Romantic? Probably not, but foolish behavior resulting in togetherness can be just as much fun.

Creating Memories with Your Sense of Taste

♥ Did you know that memories created through your sense of taste, smell, and sound last longer and are triggered more easily than those created through your sense of sight? Because of our ability to remember vividly through taste and smell, food can be used to create some rather enticing memories. On a dreary, nothing-to-make-it-special weekend afternoon, go to the market and look for four or five exotic fruits (preferably ones that neither of you have tasted). Taste test these fruits in one of the following ways:

❏ Use the fruit in sensual play. For instance, cut a mango into slices. Begin biting on one end of a slice, while your lover nibbles on the other end. Meet in the middle for a fruitful kiss.

❏ Take the fruit with you on a stroll through the park. During your walk, take turns sampling it.

❏ After blindfolding your lover, take a bite of one of the pieces of fruit. With the fruit in your mouth, kiss your blindfolded partner and see if he or she can guess the fruit. Has your mouth ever tasted so sweet? Make this a guessing game that you continue playing with many different fruits.

A Rainy Day Picnic

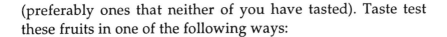 Turn a stormy day or night into a romantic situation by having an indoor picnic. Lay a blanket and some pillows on the floor next to a large window, then bring out the picnic accessories. Enjoy typical outdoor picnic foods in your warm, dry dwelling. Pour some wine and light a few candles to enhance the atmosphere. Listen to and watch the storm for a while and borrow from the intensity outside to create a moving and passionate romantic mood inside.

Change of Scenery

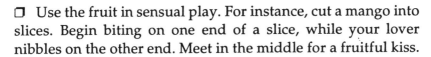 Experimenting with the unknown is often a successful ingredient for romance. Keep this in mind when selecting a restaurant. Even if you have one favorite restaurant that you frequent, try new places from time to time. Try out a new style of food—Cajun, Thai, Indian, French continental, African, vegetarian—each time you go out to dinner. This is a great way to find new favorite restaurants. Take note of those restaurants you find romantic, then return there on special occasions.

Setting the Mood

Creating a romantic mood involves appealing to all five senses. This is true whether you are planning something cozy and intimate—like reading poetry to your lover or paging through photo albums together—or something bigger, like preparing your sweetheart a five-course meal. The mood you create as the backdrop to your planned activity can do much to enhance it. All it takes is a little thought, effort, and consideration of a few mood-setting basics.

First, make sure that your surroundings are visually appealing. On the most basic level, this means that everything within view should be neat and clean. Dishes piled high in the sink and dirty socks lying on the floor will do little for a romantic mood. It also means you should do everything you can to make your surroundings extra-attractive. If you are planning a special dinner, use your best china, silver, and linens. This will show your partner how special you want him or her to feel. Also consider your choice of lighting. Almost any activity, even just watching a rented movie together, is more romantic when done by candlelight. Candlelight illuminates the one person you want to see most, while the rest of the surroundings fade into darkness. In a sense, it puts the focus on you.

To further set a romantic mood, appeal to the sense of smell. Fresh flowers are always a good choice; they add beauty as well as fragrance. Although roses are beautiful, they are not necessarily your only choice. In fact, your lover is likely to be even more impressed if you choose his or her favorite flower, or perhaps the flower that represents the month of his or her birth. For added fragrance, lightly spray a bit of perfume or cologne on any light bulbs that will be left on in the room. The heat from the bulbs will intensify the scent.

Creating the right atmosphere with background music is easy. Many people find that gentle, relaxing instrumentals and romantic *ballads are the best mood setters. However, you may decide on one of the sounds-of-nature recordings that are now available. For instance, if you want something relaxing, you can choose the sound of ocean waves crashing on the shore, or perhaps the sound of gently falling rain. If you are trying to create a tropical atmosphere, turn on the sounds of tropical birds. And one last suggestion: Try to block out or turn down any disruptive background noise, like that of the telephone.*

When appealing to your lover's sense of taste, be sure to have his or her favorite goodies on hand—cake, candy, wine, fruit, or whatever he or she enjoys the most. You can also introduce new foods to your lover, things with flavors and textures that you think he or she will enjoy. Let's say that your mate is a lover of rich chocolatey desserts, and you found a new recipe for a sinfully decadent chocolate mousse. Prepare the mousse with your sweetheart in mind, but don't simply serve it in a bowl. Instead, romantically feed it to your lover. Dip one of your fingers into the mousse, then delicately let your lover taste this delicious creation. Follow this sensuous taste test with a kiss, and maybe a sip of wine. Very slowly and sensually, continue feeding your lover from a spoon, then hand him or her one to feed you. You can be sure that whenever your lover tastes any kind of mousse again, it will conjure up romantic images of you.

The sense of touch is also important in setting the mood. A soft, fluffy blanket is perfect for wrapping yourselves in together on a cold winter night. Items such as flowing silk nightgowns, boxer shorts, and lounging robes, as well as smooth and sleek satin sheets are wonderfully sensuous to the touch.

Finally, remember that you are the focus of your lover's attention, the central figure in the mood you aim to create. Be totally aware of this as you carefully select your clothing, lingerie, and cologne or perfume. Remember to whisper loving words and offer loving touches at unexpected moments. Attention to detail is the key to creating a romantic mood. Have fun setting the stage.

Dinner Flirtations

♥ This idea, which is geared for women, is designed to drive your man crazy. For this idea, it is best to find a restaurant that is dark and romantic. When you make dinner reservations, request a table in a quiet, secluded corner. Make sure you are wearing one of your sexier outfits and some equally sexy lingerie.

Keep in mind that the very motions of eating and drinking can be extremely sensual. Once you are seated, begin your seduction. Dip one of your fingers into your cocktail, then place it sensually into your lover's mouth. Gently run your fingertips along his lips before leaning across the table for a passionate kiss. Slip off one of your shoes and glide your foot up your lover's leg, caressing him with gentle strokes. Then excuse yourself and go to the ladies room. Remove an article of lingerie (perhaps a stocking, your garter belt, or your lace panties). When you return to the table, slip the article into your lover's hand. You may never get it back. And don't be surprised if the meal doesn't last much longer. Chances are there will be stronger appetites your lover will want to satisfy.

Café Romance

♥ If you and your mate adore the intimacy of a café, try this idea at home. Set up an intimate table for two, decorate it with a candle and some flowers, and serve your favorite café beverages. Clear a small space to use as a stage and perform a poetry reading for your lover's ears only. Make use of background music to enhance this setting.

Romance from the Orient

♥ For a little sensual mystique, try dressing as a geisha for the evening. The fun in this theme comes from the attention you lavish upon your lover. Set up a full Japanese dinner (you can order out if necessary) on a low table. Have your mate remove his shoes before entering the room, and seat him on a cushion at the table. Select some distinctly mystical or Oriental background music to help set the mood. When you have finished the meal, give your lover a hot bath, followed by a massage with scented oils.

Movie Magic

♥ Recreate a romantic dinner scene from your lover's favorite movie. Make the same meal that was eaten in the movie, use the same table setting, and play the same background music. (You may even be able to buy or rent the soundtrack to the movie.) If possible, try to wear the same type of clothing as the movie characters. Rent the movie as an after-dinner attraction.

Old Fashioned Courting

♥ Rent a rowboat on a quiet lake for an afternoon. Pack a picnic basket and bring along a parasol and some music for effect. Row your lover onto the lake, or find a remote spot on shore to set up your feast. If you play an instrument, this is the perfect time for a private concert. Or you can read a romantic poem or a classic love story to your lover. You might even surprise your mate with something you have written yourself. What a wonderful way to spend a lazy afternoon.

Final Thoughts on Romantic Dinners

Be sure to take a break from the everyday routine of your lives and occasionally make mealtime a special event. Remember, with a little effort, even the simplest meal can be transformed into a romantic occasion. If you stay focused on the love you feel for your partner, romantic ideas are sure to follow. So bon appetit! Mangia! Enjoy!

11. Vacations

*V*acations offer some of the best opportunities for engaging in romance. If you were to conduct a survey and ask the question, "What are the best conditions for romance?" vacations would certainly be near the top of the list of answers. And after all, what is a honeymoon but a vacation— a vacation specifically designed to provide the perfect conditions for romance?

Vacations allow us to escape from our hectic everyday routines and to focus on our own happiness. Since time spent together is a major necessity for romance, vacations can act like romance generators. You have a span of time planned out for the two of you to do nothing but enjoy yourselves.

We must mention here that vacations are also great opportunities for taking photographs. Most couples like to keep their precious memories on film, and vacations are some of the times we want to remember most. Pictures of you and your mate will be treasured for years to come as keepsakes and as symbols of the romance that you share.

In this chapter we offer some ideas for vacations that we feel are slightly out of the ordinary. You will probably want to contact a travel agent to get more details about certain vacations, or you may simply call to get more ideas. But no matter what destination you choose, our goal is to get you thinking of ways to spend romantic time alone with your lover.

An Adventure Vacation

♥ If sightseeing all day or just lying by the pool doesn't appeal to you, perhaps an active vacation is what you need. Make your vacation an adventurous one.

All the vacations listed below can be booked through a tour operator or an outfitter. For adventure vacations, it is especially important to work with knowledgeable travel professionals, as they have the experience and expertise to lead you to an exciting but safe vacation. We've suggested a few locations that we consider outstanding for each of the various activities listed, but you may be able to find opportunities for similar activities closer to home as well. The following are ideas for adventure vacations:

❑ Go backpacking in Alaska, Vermont, or British Columbia.

❑ Bicycle across New England.

❑ Go canoeing in the Everglades, the Boundary Waters, Alaska, or northern Ontario.

❑ Go scuba diving or snorkeling in the Caribbean or off the coast of Australia.

❑ Go on a wildlife expedition in Africa, along the Amazon, or in Costa Rica.

❑ Try archaeological exploration in Mexico, Peru, or Egypt.

❑ Hike across England, the Himalayas, or the Alps.

❑ Go horseback riding in Arizona, Montana, or Alberta, Canada.

❑ Go rafting in Colorado, British Columbia, or Costa Rica.

If you prefer a more relaxing, but still active, vacation, then a theme vacation involving golf, cave exploration, bird watching, or whale watching might interest you.

The Anytime Honeymoon

♥ A lot of vacation spots and resorts cater to honeymooners and couples. These places usually have all the right stuff for the makings of a romantic vacation. It is easy to get caught up in romance in these places because they are run by people who are experts at setting the mood for you. How nice for a change! Check with your travel agent for such locations or find one yourself. Bridal magazines are good sources of information on romantic getaways. Create that magic feeling of a honeymoon every time you are on vacation.

Friendly Accommodations

♥ The place you stay on a vacation heavily influences the romantic atmosphere. Standard hotel and motel rooms may provide you with the necessities you need, but not the romantic aura. Even honeymoon suites can sometimes be a bit tacky. To get away from this, try staying in a historic inn or a bed-and-breakfast. In addition to offering more atmosphere, these establishments are often better at helping you to really get to know the area you're staying in. The extra-friendly care your hosts provide may also include insights about romantic spots nearby.

Highway Fun

♥ A key part of a romantic relationship is having fun together. If your vacation involves a long car trip, make the drive fun by creating games with romantic rewards. Here are a few examples:

❑ Make a list of things to spot and assign a romantic reward to each. Rewards could be such things as the choice of what to do at the vacation spot, a back rub, a foot massage, the choice of a movie or restaurant, and so on. The first person to spot the item gets the reward.

❒ Kiss whenever you spot a personalized license plate, a hawk, an exotic car, or anything else you decide on at the outset of the trip.

❒ Each time you spot a police car, have the passenger hand the current driver a ticket. Each ticket should specify a "penalty" of a sensual act, to be performed within twenty-four hours.

Historic Romance

♥ Many stories from history are intertwined with larger-than-life romantic episodes filled with passion and excitement. Feed off this sentiment by getting into the car and spending a romantic day at a nearby town that has a rich history and well-preserved older buildings. An old fashioned pioneer village or model historic settlement would be perfect. A visit to the town's chamber of commerce should provide you with information about the different historic sites to visit. Absorb the atmosphere of the town, and let your romantic imagination transport you back in time. This can be especially pleasant if you are used to a large, busy city.

The Secret Getaway

♥ Plan a surprise vacation to take your lover away from the humdrum of everyday life. Your destination can be as exotic as a tropical island or as simple as a hotel room in a neighboring city; the idea is to remove yourselves from your ordinary surroundings. If your mate works, make arrangements ahead of time with his or her employer for vacation time, and ask that this be kept secret in the workplace. Pack enough belongings for both of you and put them in the trunk of your car the night before you leave. The next morning, "kidnap" your lover and take him or her to your destination. To get your mate into the car, you might pretend that you're giving him or her a ride to work. If your partner isn't working that day, you'll have to invent some other pretense. Try to keep your actual destination a secret until you arrive there (or, if you must fly there, until you arrive at the airport).

Ships and Trains

❤ Take a cruise on your own love boat. Romantic places to go on a cruise include the Caribbean, the Mediterranean, Alaska, or North America's west coast. Or, if you are looking for total isolation, rent a yacht for a weekend and have a private cruise. There is no other time in your life you will be spoiled so much, and the sight of the moon rising on the horizon after a breathtaking sunset at sea will melt your heart. This is an ideal setting for passion and romance.

A variation on this idea is to take a trip by train. If possible, choose a route on which private accommodations are offered, and enjoy this most refined means of getting from here to there. Take a ride along the coast or across the state. A train ride offers the sheer rapture of watching the countryside roll by. You'll have the feeling you are reliving the romance of an old Bogart and Bacall movie. Your time together can be spent sharing thoughts and dreams, or reading to each other from a romantic classic like *Wuthering Heights*.

Spontaneous Departure

❤ Let's get down to the very basics of romance here! Romance is waking up on a Friday morning and telling your loved one that the two of you are going for a long weekend. Call your partner's employer and explain that your mate is taking the day off, and then pack a bag for two nights. Make sure to include fancy sleepwear and something nice for an elegant dinner. Drive to the bus station, train station, or airport. Go up to the window and purchase two tickets for the next departure, regardless of the destination. Once there, explore! Go sightseeing or sample different restaurants. Even if your destination turns out to be something less than a stunning success, the trip will be rewarding because you took the chance together. Spontaneity and new surroundings are vital elements of romance.

Vacations for One

♥ Are there times when your partner goes out of town on business trips or on vacations with friends? Although you will be apart, you can take advantage of the situation and have a little romantic fun, and keep your lover thinking of you despite the distance. Here are a few ideas:

❏ Pack something in your mate's luggage to remind him or her of home. A photo of you, a piece of your lingerie, a toy, a lock of hair in a fancy envelope, a picture drawn by one of your kids, or a stuffed animal will do nicely.

❏ Whether you pack for your lover or not, try to find an opportunity to slip a small gift or a letter into his or her suitcase. If you are more ambitious, place a few letters in different places in the suitcase. Write dates on the outside of the envelopes, with instructions that they are not to be opened until the proper date. Be imaginative in how you use the letters. For example, you can make a game out of it, tell a story, or create a puzzle or mystery.

❏ Arrange to have a gift, letter, flowers, or a small bottle of wine sent to the hotel where your lover is staying. Ask that a little note be attached that reads, "I'm thinking of you."

❏ If your spouse is on a business trip and you want to really create a surprise, make arrangements to get into the hotel room where he or she is staying. Proceed to set up a candlelight affair, with champagne, flowers, etc. If possible, make arrangements with your loved one's coworkers to get him or her back to the hotel room at an appropriate time. When your partner comes back from the day's business meetings, everything will be set up for a surprise romantic evening.

❏ If you are the one who has to travel and spend time apart from your loved one, you can take this opportunity to send home some romantic fun. The idea here is to send a puzzle, using postcards as the pieces. Assemble a number of postcards (enough so that you can send one each day while you are away) and place them next to each other, forming a large square or rectangle. With a large marker, write a love message in such a way that each postcard contains at least a little bit of writing. Then send the postcards, one at a time and in a random fashion, for your mate to unscramble. Even though you can't be there, you will still be in your lover's thoughts.

❏ If you must take frequent business trips, you can make your sweetheart's day by secretly leaving a flower or note on his or her pillow before you leave. A habit like this will show your consideration and love for your partner, even when you can't be there.

❏ Call your lover and say, "I love you," or leave this message on the answering machine. Sometimes this simplest of gestures really says it best.

Welcome Home

♥ If your lover goes away without you, regardless of the reason, have a special welcome ready when he or she gets back. If you are married, make sure to be there when your spouse arrives. If you have children, have them there as well, if possible. A happy family greeting is a nice gesture to come back to, especially if you are not used to being away from home. Have a home-cooked meal of favorite foods waiting.

While your partner is away, tape his or her favorite television shows and save any newspapers and mail that was collected. Have these items set aside to be looked at later when there is time.

After dinner, prepare to take your lover to heaven with a sensuous massage. Next you might furnish a soothing bath or hot tub. If the two of you have any energy left by this time, show how much you missed your mate with lots of kisses and love. What a way to be welcomed home!

Winter Resort Town

♥ When most people think of a vacation, they think of relaxing on a hot beach. Few people consider a vacation in a winter resort town, especially if they don't ski. But a vacation in a snowy paradise can be very romantic. You can ice-skate hand in hand outdoors, go dog-sledding across a frozen lake, walk through a picturesque snowfall, go snowmobiling, toboggan down a hill, build a snowman, make snow angels, have a playful snowball fight, or visit a winter festival. When the day is over, you can cuddle up in front of a fire with a mug of hot chocolate or a glass of wine. The advantage of this type of vacation is the cozy and intimate atmosphere, which is ideally suited to romantic expression.

Almost Home

♥ If a visit to a tropical island or a foreign country is out of the question, why not take advantage of a local resort in your area? There is probably a vacation resort somewhere within a few hours' drive of your home. This idea allows you to get away from your everyday surroundings, and usually at less expense. Or you can try visiting a casino resort. Even if you don't gamble, the luxurious accomodations and surrounding scenery often allow for private romantic getaways.

Go Into Hiding

♥ If you are looking for time alone with your partner, but you don't have much money to spend on a vacation, you can kidnap your lover at home. Stock up on your favorite foods, buy some candles, and make sure you have plenty of romantic music and videos on hand. Then hide the phone and turn down the volume on the answering machine. If anyone inquires, say that you are going away for a few days. You and your mate are officially in hiding!

You can expand on the idea of travelling without leaving home by using recordings of nature sounds, available at most music stores. You can "go" to a different place each day by listening to waves crashing on the beach, the sounds of wildlife in the rain forests, or the sounds of a glacier melting. Whatever theme you choose, the important point is that you enjoy your time alone together.

Final Thoughts on Vacations

A vacation can mean much more than sleeping late and taking some time away from the demands of work. It can be the perfect opportunity to recharge your romantic relationship.

It doesn't matter whether you prefer to spend your vacation sightseeing, having an outdoor adventure, or lazing by the pool. With the right approach, any of these vacations can be romantic, because they have one important thing in common: They give you time to spend with your lover and away from daily distractions. This allows you to truly focus on each other. No matter where you take your vacation, your vacation can take you to a special romantic world, a world where the only people that matter are you and your mate. We guarantee you'll come back re-energized, and eager to find new ways to continue your romantic adventure together.

When Ending
Your Love Letter. . .

After you have taken the time to write a passionate love note or letter to your partner, don't sign off with an ordinary ending. Consider using one of the following special expressions of love to end your heartfelt message:

Ever yours, my love,

Hopelessly devoted,

Your lover,

Yours with much love,

All my love now and forever,

With dearest love,

Adieu, my dear heart,

Wish I could kiss you,

From now on, all yours,

I kiss you,

Your devoted __(name)__

Ever affectionately,

Passionately yours,

Your ever-faithful lover,

Ever yours, ever faithfully,

With burning love in my heart,

I am yours,

Raging with desire for you,

With intoxicating love,

With you in spirit,

You are my endless love,

Always yours in passion,

With limitless love,

In a frenzy over thoughts of you,

Desiring only you,

I love you with my whole heart,

I shall love you always,

Your beloved,

With longing for you,

My heart is yours,

Till I am home in your arms,

Heaven bless you,

You are the breath of my life,

I wish I were in your arms,

Love forever and a day,

You make me whole,

12. Everyday
Expressions of Love

C reativity and awareness are two main points that we have stressed throughout this book, and with good reason; they are essential for romance. We want you to be able to create special romantic moments out of ordinary ones. Our goal is to get you thinking romantically as often as possible.

To be able to take any given moment or day and tune in to its romantic possibilities requires creativity. There is romantic potential in virtually everything. The key is to train yourself to look for creative ideas even while engaged in primarily practical activities. For instance, be on the lookout for romantic ideas when you are doing such ordinary things as flipping through newspapers or magazines, going shopping, looking through the yellow pages or travel brochures, or doing any other everyday activity. Any of these can trigger ideas for romantic opportunities. Sometimes all you have to do is find ways to be alone together, which will lead to the kind of romantic quality time that is so very important.

In this chapter we have included some tools for introducing romance into your life anytime, anywhere. It often will be apparent that the simple act of being together in quiet comfort can be intensely romantic. Make this your goal, and your quality of life is sure to benefit.

Movie Magic

♥ One of the things that is vital for romantic encounters is the mood. It is difficult to be fully open to your partner if you are not in the right frame of mind. One way to set the proper mood is to watch a romantic movie, preferably by candlelight and while in each other's arms. You can watch an old classic, like *Wuthering Heights; Romeo and Juliet; Casablanca; An Affair to Remember; Now, Voyager; Camille; The Way We Were; Somewhere in Time; Love Story;* or *West Side Story,* or something more recent like *Ghost; An Officer and a Gentleman; Chances Are; Pretty Woman; Enchanted April; It Could Happen to You; Sleepless in Seattle;* or *When Harry Met Sally.* This is a wonderful way to establish a loving mood.

Games of Love

♥ Have some fun and play a game for two with romantic rewards involved. You can do this by modifying the rules of any board game or card game, or by making up your own game. Some of the rewards can include giving back and/or foot massages; preparing breakfast in bed; promising to do something, such as a household chore, that you usually avoid; watching a movie of your spouse's choice together; preparing a family dinner; and so on. For example, if you are playing Monopoly, you can use your own romantic reward cards in place of the Chance and Community Chest cards. You can also assign a dollar value to each of the romantic rewards and buy these favors with the game money at specified times during or at the end of the game.

For a more ambitious game that works well for long car trips, devise a personalized road rally. Make a list of things to search for as you drive, and decide on a romantic favor for each. For example, you might decide that the first person to spot a barn with a white roof will receive breakfast in bed. The fun part in playing these games is that it may take days or months to complete them, since they aren't really over until all the rewards are fulfilled.

The Wheel of Love

♥ This idea is a nice variation on the *Games of Love* idea (page 174). The main difference is in the presentation. You will need two pieces of large poster board and a pin or fastener. You will also have to collaborate to make a list of romantic activities. Then, cut one piece of poster board into a large circle. Using a marker, divide the circle into as many pie-shaped sections as you have activities, and write one activity in each space. Next, place this circle in the center of the other piece of poster board. Secure the circle in the center with a pin or fastener that allows the circle to spin. At the top of the large piece of poster board, make an arrow pointing downward toward the circle (or perhaps a heart with its bottom point serving as the arrow). When your partner spins the wheel, the offer that ends up directly under the arrow is the one you must fulfill. If you want, you can draw two hearts that point toward the wheel, one with each of your names on it. This way, every time the wheel is spun, you both win.

Be creative and decorate your wheel of love with drawings, ribbons, gift wrap, colored poster board, illustrations cut out of magazines or old greeting cards, or heart-shaped candies. You can also write a message on the back board, perhaps something like "I love you so much, I would _____ for you!" (Write this so that the blank is filled in by the romantic activity that wins the spin.) Or you could simply write "I love you" across the board.

Set aside one day each week or every other week to spin the wheel and make good on your offers. In addition to being a fun game for both of you, this wheel is something you can save and use again and again. You can even collaborate to make new prizes to spin for. So let your lover spin the wheel, and let luck take over.

Play Fights

♥ It's time for some fun. Bring out Mr. Bubble and have a bubble bath fight. Whenever water is involved, interesting romantic results may ensue. Other fun play fights may involve the use of squirt guns, water balloons, or pillows.

In addition to being fun, play fights can relieve stress and tension, things that make romance difficult on a daily basis. Doing fun things together is vital to all relationships and reminds you to smile. It has been medically proven that smiling is good for you. A sincere smile also radiates your warmth and love of life—a very attractive quality.

Togetherness

♥ The time you spend with your partner is important. If it's becoming mundane, then perhaps you should consider participating in an activity together. When a couple takes part in an activity together, it gives them more in common, more shared experiences, and more to talk about. Having a common interest helps in the enjoyment of a relationship. Every activity has its own rewards; here are a few possibilities:

❏ Expand your interests and attend classes together. Take lessons in creative subjects like art, dancing, photography, acting, or cooking, or learn a sport like golf or tennis together.

❏ Join a club together. Book clubs, sports and fitness organizations, church groups, and nature clubs are good choices.

❏ Take part in a community play together. If you are not comfortable with acting, there are many other ways you can participate, such as working on scenery, lighting, costumes, makeup, or music.

❐ Together, volunteer to help a worthy cause. You might consider involvement with:

* An environmental group such as Greenpeace or the World Wildlife Fund.
* A youth group or local kids' sports team.
* Your local civic association.
* An outreach project such as a food bank or a soup kitchen.
* A local hospital or nursing home.
* Your local Red Cross chapter.
* A health-related organization such as the American Cancer Society or the Muscular Dystrophy Foundation.
* Scouting organizations.
* Big Brother/Sister programs.
* Child Find or other like organizations.
* A social welfare or advocacy organization such as the Salvation Army or Amnesty International.
* A cultural organization such as a museum or historical society.

Love at Your Fingertips

If you and your partner are into sensual experiences, you will probably find nothing more fulfilling than massage. This isn't something you have to be a professional to perform. Just ask each other what feels good. There are also many easy-to-follow books and videos available on the subject (check a bookstore or your local public library). Try doing massage on different parts of the body, such as the face, back, shoulders, feet, hands, and legs, and experiment with the use of different oils and powders. Pull out all the stops to create an ideal setting when giving a massage—put on soft, relaxing music, light some candles, and perfume the air with incense. When you truly love the person you are concentrating this energy on, you will enjoy giving a massage as much as receiving one.

Or consider giving your lover a scalp massage. You have probably had your hair washed by a hairdresser at some point in your life. Remember how unbelievably relaxing and enjoyable it felt? For the same effect, you can simply run your fingers through your lover's hair while gently scratching and massaging his or her scalp. Or, some evening while you are watching a movie or catching the late show, ask if your partner would like to have his or her hair brushed. Put all your care and love into a slow, gentle brushing. For the full treatment, follow this with a sensual shampoo. The result should be a very loving, relaxed mood.

Bath Time

♥ Here is a simple yet sensual idea for you and your lover. Take a long, hot bubble bath in a room bathed in candlelight and soothing music. You and your partner can have some fun in the tub by playing with bathtub crayons and rubber duckies. Or you can keep the setting more straightforwardly romantic by floating roses on the bath water and placing aromatic devices such as incense or scented candles around the room. You can also lightly spray some perfume in the room for an aromatic touch. The atmosphere can be further enhanced by placing a vase of flowers next to the bathtub or by hanging bunches of dried flowers in the corners of the room.

Use the hot bath or Jacuzzi idea as a surprise whenever your spouse could use a relaxing moment alone with you. Next to the tub, set up drinks and a snack, like wine with fresh fruit or cheese and crackers. This idea is also extremely thoughtful for anytime your partner has had a hard day at work or has spent long hours working in the backyard, or when you just want to give him or her a break from everyday hassles.

A Marriage Experience

♥ If you and your lover aren't married, it can be very romantic to do something as simple as going grocery shopping, cooking, or gardening together. Playing the role of a married couple can give you new perspective on your commitment and on the importance of your relationship.

Another possibility is taking a young niece or nephew out for the afternoon. Go out for some ice cream, play miniature golf, or go to the zoo. This can be a thoroughly stimulating experience for the child, and it can give you a glimpse of your own future family together.

Married, With Children

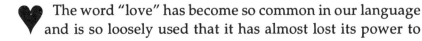 If you have children, it is important to have some private time as a couple. It may require determination and careful planning to free up time for yourselves. Arrange to have a baby sitter from time to time, even if for no other reason than to be alone together. Use the time however you wish, but include some quality time for talk, romance, and other activities that solidify your bond. Each of you can write down a fantasy and then read it to the other. This allows you to share your romantic thoughts and create a perfect romantic atmosphere.

Love and Laughter

From the serious we now shift to the simple and downright goofy. Have you been in a public place and found yourself bursting into laughter for the simplest or silliest of reasons? The laughter continued until your companion finally started laughing, too, and after a while, you were both laughing so hard that stopping was out of the question. The next time you and your mate are in a restaurant or other public place, have a little competition to try to get each other laughing. The one who loses must pay a romantic price. Very silly, but very lovable.

A Substitute for Love

The word "love" has become so common in our language and is so loosely used that it has almost lost its power to

Flowers and Their Meanings

Sending flowers is a beautiful gesture all by itself, but to add a little extra meaning, choose flowers whose traditional meanings coincide with the message or feeling you want to convey. The list below indicates the meaning of some popular flowers.

Flower	Traditional Meaning
Aster	Talisman of love
Begonia	A fanciful nature
Bellflower, white	Gratitude
Carnation, pink	Emblem of Mother's Day
Carnation, red	Admiration
Carnation, white	Pure and ardent love
Chrysanthemum, red	I love you
Chrysanthemum, white	Truth
Cockscomb	Affection
Daffodil	Regard
Daisy	Innocence, gentleness
Forget-me-not	True love
Globe amaranth	Unfading love
Heliotrope	Devotion

Flower	Traditional Meaning
Hibiscus	Delicate beauty
Honesty	Honesty
Jasmine, white	Amiability
Jasmine, yellow	Modesty
Larkspur	An open heart
Lily of the valley	Purity and humility
Pansy	Thoughtful recollection
Peony	Healing
Phlox	Sweet dreams
Primrose	Young love
Rose, pink	Perfect happiness
Rose, red	Love and desire
Rose, white	Charm and innocence
Rose, white and red	Unity
Rosebud	Beauty and youth
Sunflower	Homage and devotion
Sweet alyssum	Worth beyond beauty
Tuberose	Dangerous pleasures
Tulip	You are the perfect lover
Verbena	May you get your wish
Violet	Modesty and simplicity

convey the strong emotions it is really associated with. One idea with the potential for great impact is to devise your own personalized word for "love" that is stronger and more intimately connected to your relationship with each other. This word should inspire passionate and romantic feelings whenever it is spoken, and should signal you to think about or act on your love.

Another way to develop your own personal language of love is to learn to say "I love you" in American Sign Language, or to develop your own signs. This way you can send out your feelings to each other across a crowded room or in any other situation. Or you can learn to express your emotions in other languages. These are wonderful ways to keep your reminders of love special.

A Peek Into the Crystal Ball

♥ Visit a fortuneteller together. You can have your palms, tarot cards, or tea leaves read, or you can speak with a psychic. A visit to such a soothsayer can provide heightened excitement and romantic interest. Fortunetellers specialize in stories of love, because love is an integral part of the human experience that concerns all of us. However, you must first promise each other that this is only for fun, and not to be taken too seriously. Trying to discover your future through different mediums can be fun as well as romantic. You can also pretend to read your mate's palm or tea leaves. Make sure to "see" yourself in your mate's future!

Sharing Unique Experiences

♥ Fresh, exciting new experiences keep a relationship healthy. From time to time, make a point of doing something that you normally wouldn't do or that you have never done before. You and your partner will have an amusing time when it comes to sharing first experiences. It doesn't have to be something extraordinary, just something you don't ordinarily do together. Here are a few possibilities:

❑ Go to the library and take out a book of plays. Divide up the parts and then act out a play together. Beware, though; this can become very comical!

❑ Have a private singing party. Play the music to some of your favorite songs and sing along together. It doesn't matter if you don't have a great voice; the point is to have fun. If either of you can play an instrument, this experience can be even better.

❑ Take ballroom dancing lessons together, and practice what you've learned at home. As simple as it is, a waltz around the kitchen after dinner can be very romantic.

❑ Arrange to take a ride in a private plane or helicopter. This will let you see the city you live in from a rousing new perspective.

❑ Go for a hot air balloon ride. Bring some champagne and something to eat and have a party aboard. Seeing things from a fresh perspective will give you and your lover a feeling of exhiliration and freedom.

Here are a few more activities you might consider if you have never done them together or if it's been some time since you tried them:

❑ Take a winery tour.

❑ Listen to music together in complete darkness.

❑ Spend an evening with only candles lighting your abode.

❑ Watch a sunrise together.

❑ Shop at as many flea markets as you can in one day.

❑ Stroll through a botanical garden or greenhouse.

❑ Browse in antique stores.

❑ Spend a day at a music festival, whether folk, jazz, blues, classical, or pop.

❑ Get wet at a water park or go to an amusement park.

❏ Go ice-skating, roller-skating, or roller-blading.

❏ Play bingo.

❏ Play strip poker (or adapt the basic concept using any other game).

❏ Give your husband a shave.

❏ Visit a zoo.

❏ Go camping.

❏ Play billiards in a pool hall.

❏ Take a tour in a double-decker bus.

❏ Go strawberry- or apple-picking.

❏ Participate in an auction.

❏ Rent a rowboat and have lunch in the middle of a lake.

❏ Go canoeing across a lake or down a river.

❏ Go hiking in the woods.

❏ Toboggan down a hill.

Romantic Characters

♥ If you have an interest in acting, plan a day with a theatrical flair. You and your mate can assume personalities from literature, history, cinema, opera, the theater, or the Bible. Any romantic couple from history or the world of make-believe is perfect for this. Do it right; dress up and stay in character through an entire day or evening. Possible costume ideas include knights and princesses, ancient Romans, cavemen, kings and queens, ancient Egyptians, Victorians, or tropical island natives. Assume your characters all day if possible, at least through dinner and into the bedroom. A little unusual, but you may be amazed at the effect role-playing can have. It is a very liberating feeling and great fun!

Expressions of Love

♥ Poetry! Many consider it the purest form of romantic expression. The combination of a sincere and impassioned voice and the right setting can touch any heart. The main thing is to pick a poet whose work you feel comfortable with and find moving, and to combine this with an appropriate activity or setting. So many of the activities mentioned throughout this book can benefit from the inclusion of poetry, but we will mention a few specific ones here. Examples include sitting in front of a fireplace (even better if it's in a log cabin in the woods), cuddling up in a room aglow with many candles, giving a massage, going out in a boat at night with only the moon for a light, sitting on a beach next to a fire, or going up to the top of a tall building and looking out over the town below. Any somewhat isolated location can provide the privacy required for poetic professions of love.

Most bookstores or libraries will have books of love poems, but if you are unsure of what to look for, here is a short list of poets to investigate:

- ❑ W.H. Auden
- ❑ William Blake
- ❑ Rupert Brooke
- ❑ Elizabeth Barrett Browning
- ❑ Robert Browning
- ❑ Robert Burns
- ❑ Lord Byron
- ❑ E.E. Cummings
- ❑ Emily Dickinson
- ❑ John Donne
- ❑ T.S. Eliot
- ❑ Robert Frost
- ❑ Robert Graves
- ❑ Robert Herrick
- ❑ John Keats
- ❑ Omar Khayyam
- ❑ Rod McKuen
- ❑ Andrew Marvell
- ❑ Edna St. Vincent Millay
- ❑ John Milton
- ❑ Sir Walter Raleigh
- ❑ Rumi
- ❑ William Shakespeare

☐ Percy Bysshe Shelley   ☐ William Wordsworth

☐ Alfred, Lord Tennyson   ☐ William Butler Yeats

☐ William Carlos Williams

Music is the Food of Love

♥ As with the *Expressions of Love* idea (page 185), you can use classical or other music that the two of you find romantic to set an inspiring and tender mood. A short list of some of the best classical pieces includes the following:

☐ Sonata No. 14 in C-sharp minor ("Moonlight Sonata") by Ludwig van Beethoven.

☐ *Carmen* by Georges Bizet.

☐ "Peer Gynt Suites" by Edvard Grieg.

☐ "Liebesträume (Three Nocturnes for Piano)" or "Les Préludes (Symphonic Poem No. 3)" by Franz Liszt.

☐ *A Midsummer Night's Dream* by Felix Mendelssohn.

☐ *Le nozze de Figaro (The Marriage of Figaro)* or *Così fan tutte* by Wolfgang Amadeus Mozart.

☐ "Canon and Gigue in D" by Johann Pachelbel.

☐ *Romeo and Juliet* by Sergei Prokofiev.

☐ "Rhapsody on a Theme of Paganini" by Sergei Rachmaninoff.

☐ "Boléro" by Maurice Ravel.

☐ "Trois Gymnopédies" by Erik Satie.

☐ Symphony No. 8 in B minor ("Unfinished") by Franz Schubert.

☐ *Swan Lake; Sleeping Beauty;* or *The Nutcracker* by Pyotr Ilyich Tchaikovsky.

☐ *December* by George Winston.

Intimate Bedtime Stories

♥ If you are a natural storyteller, you can use this talent to give a marvelous romantic gift to your partner. Tell him or her a bedtime story. The story can be purely fictional or it can have connections to the true story of your love affair. Regardless of your character choice, the premise here is romance. Use candles, scents, and romantic lighting to enhance the effect of your tale. Can you think of a better way to send your partner off to dreamland?

If you are not the type to make up your own stories, you can have nightly readings from a classic romantic novel like *Wuthering Heights, Middlemarch, Jane Eyre, Pride and Prejudice,* or any other book that is a particular favorite. Make this a daily romantic ritual, and give yourselves something special to look forward to each evening.

Romantic Stories

♥ Peeking into the romantic lives of other couples can be interesting and a lot of fun. Reading allows us glimpses into the private lives of people we otherwise would never know. Sometimes their examples can inspire us with new romantic ideas. There are several good books on the market that allow you to read about romance among famous historical people. You and your partner can do this while at a park, a beach, or at home in bed.

Here are a few books to look for:

❐ *Love Letters* by Antonia Fraser—actual love letters from famous couples in history.

❐ *Noble Lovers* by D.D.R. Owen—tales of well-known pairs of lovers in history.

❐ *The Voice of the Middle Ages in Personal Letters 1100–1500* by Catherine Moriarty.

A variation on this idea is to read parts of dime-store romance novels to each other every evening. Often, just reading about romance can supply the creative stimulus required to energize your own relationship.

Romantic Reminders

♥ This is the simplest idea you are likely to find in this book, but we promise that little else will match it for effectiveness. If you are out of town or out of the house, telephone your mate and say "I love you!" and hang up before he or she has a chance to respond. This can be done anywhere and at any time. It's such a simple reminder, but it really says it all.

Love Letters

♥ A hand-written, private letter to the one you love has always been one of the most purely romantic gestures. It is sublimely moving to let another person completely permeate your thoughts as you pour your love onto the written page. Take any opportunity you can to send a letter of love, and remember that a letter sent for no occasion at all will make the greatest impact. If you are running low on ideas for romantic expression, remember that analogies are a good way of getting your point across. Use stories (possibly from novels) in your letter that parallel the point you want to make. Other ideas to make your letter interesting include:

❑ Write on scented stationery and seal your letter with a kiss or sealing wax.

❑ Write out your letter in calligraphy.

❑ Record your message on an audiocassette or videotape.

❑ Stuff your letter into a balloon to be blown up or filled with helium.

❑ Write your message of love on a slip of paper and insert it in a fortune cookie.

❏ Cut a letter into pieces to be reconstructed as a jigsaw puzzle.

❏ Write your message in puzzle form (such as a cryptogram or crossword) with clues for your lover to solve it.

❏ Make a long banner with romantic embellishments and hang it up.

❏ Leave a message on your lover's computer screen. If you can manage to do this at his or her workplace, the gesture will have even greater surprise potential.

❏ Put special things like confetti, small candies, perfume samples, flower petals, or perhaps a small picture in your letter.

❏ Set a message in a bottle afloat in your pool, or in a small lake or pond where you know your lover will find it.

Culture of Romance

♥ If you live in or near a large city, consider yourself lucky. True love is an enduring theme in many of the classical arts and cultural activities. Fine dining, the ballet, the opera or symphony, the theater, and ballroom dancing are costlier but more intense ways to experience romance with the one you love. The fine arts are among the best vehicles for setting free your deepest and most passionate feelings.

Romantic Escapades

♥ A sure-fire way to bring you and your lover closer is to get involved in an adventure together. There are many companies that offer adventure experiences like white-water rafting, bicycling, or mountain trekking. In addition, many public parks provide opportunities for hiking, canoeing, scuba diving, and many other outdoor adventures. You might not think of these activities as romantic, but remember that togetherness and shared experiences are the basic building blocks of romance. Cuddling around a campfire and roasting marshmallows, while discussing the past day's canoe trip, is positively romantic. So go ahead and make an adventure for yourself.

What Are You Doing Friday Night?

♥ A little break from the ordinary can be achieved by asking your wife or husband for a date. Many couples express a desire to relive the romance, excitement, and uncertainty of a new encounter. Show up at your house at a designated time, pretending that you don't actually live there. With royal ceremony, pick up your spouse and go out for a date similar to one of your first ones. Relive your early date through role-playing. Reach back and conjure up memories of the time when your love was brand-new.

Another variation on the dating theme is to act as a team to come up with a complete date. So that the responsibility for coming up with a date that is fun for both parties does not fall exclusively on one person, have each partner devise plans for different phases of the evening. For example, you might select a restaurant for dinner, while your partner decides where to go afterward for entertainment. Alternate planning chores until you piece together a full date.

Staying Romantic

♥ Over time, it is easy to become complacent in a relationship and unimaginitive about your romantic activities. Except on special occasions, you may rarely do anything to spice up your life. To get out of these romantic doldrums, get into the habit of writing down romantic ideas on your calendar or daily planner on random days throughout the year. Even if you just draw a heart on a specific day a few months from now, this can serve as a reminder that you should be setting aside time to romance your mate. When your partner is feeling low, use this as reason to do something cheery or romantic. Do something small, like giving flowers or a card for no reason at all. Or, if you have more time on your hands, do something more elaborate. Anything you do will surely be appreciated and move you in the right direction.

Romantic Strolls

♥ Going for a walk together is one of the simplest ways to be romantic. Whether you plan your outing in advance or do it spontaneously, this quiet time together can be quite precious. So consider your surrounding area and imagine the most serene place to share your romantic fantasies. Go walking near a lake, along a beach, or through a park, historical town, or botanical garden. A simple stroll around your neighborhood is a good choice, too. You might choose to take your walk at sunrise or sunset, under the stars, or in the rain or snow. It doesn't matter where or when you decide to take your walk. The main idea here is to get out and away from the distractions of home life, and to allow yourselves time to dream together.

Constellation Concentration

♥ On a clear night, grab a blanket and your sweetheart, and find a good spot to do some stargazing. Bring along some wine and glasses, lie back, and enjoy each other's company. Try using a glow-in-the-dark map of the constellations to find the ones that represent your astrological signs. Or bring along a radio and do a little slow dancing under the stars.

Guess Who?

♥ Playing the secret admirer for your mate is a great way to raise his or her spirits. This is a simple technique for reminding your partner of how wonderful you think he or she is, and why your love runs so deep. Write anonymous notes to your partner (use a typewriter or try to disguise your handwriting). Have each note express a different reason why your lover makes you smile. And don't just send notes; send flowers, candy, balloons, little volumes of love poetry, or whatever your partner is fond of. When you notice that your mate is about to burst with curiosity, send a note stating that you will be waiting to meet him or her in a particular spot at a specific time. Imagine your lover's delight when you reveal the secret—you!

Romance is Alive and Well

♥ It can be hard to be romantic all the time, but it helps if you get into the habit of reminding yourself why your partner makes you smile. This alone should keep you going, and remind you to make him or her smile. Here are a few ideas to keep you in your lover's thoughts:

❐ Draw a picture and write a love message with water-based markers on the bathroom mirror in the morning.

❐ Sneak into the bathroom while your partner is in the shower and write "I love you" in the mist on the mirror.

❐ Put a message in her makeup case that mentions how beautiful she is to you, with or without makeup.

❐ If it's winter, you can write a welcome message in the frost or dew of a window or door.

❐ Do one of your partner's daily chores before he or she has a chance to.

❐ If you pass by someone selling flowers, buy some for your mate.

❐ Put a love note in with your partner's lunch, or between the inner and outer caps of a Thermos bottle.

❐ Fill the medicine cabinet with flower petals or candy.

❐ Prepare breakfast in bed every so often.

❐ Place a flower or a love note on your lover's dinner plate or breakfast setting.

❐ Make heart-shaped pancakes instead of round ones, perhaps topped with two or three strawberry halves (sliced from top to bottom so that they too are heart-shaped).

☐ Prepare a relaxing scented bath for your partner.

Final Thoughts on Expressing Your Love Every Day

Romance is *not* just for special occasions. Once you make the decision to increase the level of romance in your life, you'll find hundreds of possibilities open to you.

All you have to do is get into the habit of thinking, as often as possible, of the reasons you love your partner, and then look for ways to express your feelings. Your romantic gestures can be as simple as a loving word or note or as grand as a surprise vacation—anything that makes your mate feel special and shows how much you care. Once you get into the habit, you'll find yourself waking up each day to a brand-new opportunity for romance.

Conclusion

N

ow that you have journeyed through our wonderful world of romance, you can sit back and reflect on your trip. We hope you have enjoyed reading our romantic suggestions, but more importantly, we hope you have learned how to "turn on" your romantic instincts. The ideas included in this book are intended to encourage your romantic creativity, and get your thoughts moving in the direction of your lover. These ideas are also intended to help you get a feel for how to inject romance into almost any situation.

Throughout this book we have stressed the importance of focusing on your partner and being creative, but the most important element in romance is thoughtfulness. Every romantic gesture you make, no matter how small, shows your partner that you are thinking of him or her, which is the most romantic thing you can do. In turn, your actions keep you on your lover's mind, which can create a wonderful chain reaction of reciprocated romantic actions—a rather pleasant side effect.

Think of our suggestions as springboards toward more personalized actions. We are aware that you have your own ideas about what romance should be, so be prepared to alter the ideas we have given you to suit your own relationship. Think about the best times you have shared, and about the times you would like to share in the future. You can set the tone for future romance by making subtle changes in your actions now.

Whether you have just started dating your partner or you are already partners for life, romance should be an important part of your relationship—a habit you should never want to break.

Part III

Your Personal Romantic Reference

Throughout this book we have stressed the importance of thinking ahead, making mental notes of specific information and incidents, and putting thought into romance in general. For instance, we have encouraged you to note such things as the place and date you and your partner first met, names of restaurants the two of you have enjoyed, and all of your partner's personal favorite things. Part III is designed as a reference for keeping track of these important bits of information.

With all of this information on hand, you can make any romantic gesture just a touch more thoughtful. For example, you can use your partner's favorite color for the ribbon on a gift, add a favorite drink to your romantic table setting, or insert a "remember when" note in a card. Part III is designed to help you along with such special touches.

Fill out the lists on the following pages to the best of your ability. It's best to fill in the blanks as you come upon information, so you don't have to wheedle information out of your partner right before you are planning a surprise. You may also want to add some notes and little reflections to the facts you record here, like what your partner was wearing the first time you laid eyes on him or her. And don't be shy about adding any definite dislikes your partner has toward certain foods, fragrances, or just about anything else. Also be sure to make note of allergies or other sensitivites your partner may have.

This personal reference section can be extremely helpful in several areas. However, it won't help you unless you fill it out first. So grab a pen and get to work!

IMPORTANT DATES

If you tend to forget special dates easily, it's nice to have them together for quick reference.

Partner's birthday: _____

First encounter: _____

First date: _____

First kiss: _____

Night of the proposal: _____

Wedding day: _____

1st child's birthday: _____

2nd child's birthday:_____

3rd child's birthday: _____

4th child's birthday: _____

In-laws' birthdays: _____

Significant others: _____

_____

_____

_____

WORK SCHEDULE

It's a good idea to have your partner's work schedule handy to plan for surprises or phone calls. We have included this list because your mate may be one of those people whose schedule changes periodically, or you simply may have trouble remembering.

Work address: _____

Work phone number: _____

	Mon	**Tue**	**Wed**	**Thur**	**Fri**	**Sat**	**Sun**

Start: _____

Lunch: _____

Breaks: _____

Finish: _____

Arrival
at home: _____

Vacation: _____

_____

FAVORITES LIST

It is important for you to remember your partner's favorite things. Although you have probably made a mental note of these things, it can't hurt to write them down. Your partner's tastes may change, so be sure to update your list from time to time. And remember, your partner may have more than one favorite item in each space, or he or she may not have a "favorite" for some things at all. Use this list when buying a gift, preparing dinner, buying flowers, choosing a movie, or for any other romantic gesture.

Favorite color: _____

Favorite flower: _____

Favorite jewelry (metal, style): _____

Favorite stone: _____

Favorite perfume or cologne: _____

Lucky number: _____

Favorite restaurant: _____

Favorite food: _____

Favorite wine: _____

Favorite liqueur: _____

Favorite drink: _____

Favorite dessert: _____

Favorite ice cream: _____

Favorite cake: _____

Favorite fruit: _____

Favorite vegetable: _____

Favorite pizza toppings: _____

Favorite snack food: _____

Favorite cartoon character: _____

Favorite comic strip: _____

Favorite author: _____

Favorite romantic poet: _____

Favorite song: _____

Favorite singer or band: _____

Favorite comedian: _____

Favorite TV show: _____

Favorite sports hero: _____

Favorite sport to watch: _____

Favorite sport to play: _____

Hobbies and interests: _____

WHAT'S YOUR SIZE?

It's a good idea to keep a list of your partner's clothing and jewelry sizes on hand when buying gifts. If your partner is a little touchy about this type of thing, you may have to get creative, perhaps wrapping a piece of string around his or her finger playfully to get a ring size, or peeking at tag to get a clothing size. For obvious reasons, you don't want to have to guess at your partner's size when shopping for a gift.

Coat size: _____

Dress size: _____

Glove size: _____

Hat size: _____

Jacket size: _____

Neck size:_____

Pants size: _____

Ring size: _____

Shirt size: _____

Shoe size:_____

Suit size:_____

Sweater size: _____

Underwear size:_____

Other: _____

ROMANTIC RESTAURANTS

Whenever you come across a restaurant that you consider romantic, write it down on this list. Make a note of what was so special about this place, perhaps the food, the lighting, or the background music. To be sure of the restaurant's address and phone number, you might take a napkin or matchbook from the restaurant that has an imprint of this information. As soon as possible, add this information to the list below. It will come in handy on special occasions.

Restaurant/Address/Phone   **Comments**

WHY I LOVE YOU

This list is a romantic reminder of all of the reasons you fell in love with your partner, and why you have continued to love him or her over the years. You might use this list as a reminder of your faith in your mate after you have had an argument or while you are going through bad times. You can also refer to this list when you are trying to find just the right sentiment to write in a note or card.

I love you because . . .

_____

_____

_____

_____

_____

_____

_____

_____

_____

_____

_____

_____

_____

WEDDING VOWS

Your wedding vows serve as a romantic reminder of a very special day in your lives, as well as a perfect reference for romantic notes and cards. Fill in your vows here to reflect on the faith and love in your marriage.

_____

_____

_____

_____

_____

_____

_____

_____

_____

_____

_____

_____

_____

_____

_____

PERSONAL RESOLUTIONS

All of us would like to better ourselves in one way or another.
This includes improving our relationships. Fill in the lists below with your ideas on how you can better contribute to your
relationship. Review this list periodically as a reminder of your
goals.

Things I want to do more of: _____

_____

_____

_____

_____

Things I want to do less of:_____

_____

_____

_____

_____

Things I want to continue doing:_____

_____

_____

_____

_____

NEW ROMANTIC IDEAS

The purpose of this book is to give you creative, romantic options for any occasion. Simply scan through the book for an idea you like, and either use it or modify it to fit your own situation. This is much easier than developing an idea from scratch each and every time. That is why you should get into the habit of writing down any new ideas you come up with or hear of. Jot these ideas, or variations of ideas, in the space below. It will give you more options when scanning through this book.

_____

_____

_____

_____

_____

_____

_____

_____

_____

_____

_____

_____

SPECIAL MOMENTS

You probably have a few special memories that don't fit into other lists but that are very much worth writing down. These special remembrances can help you when writing love letters and creating personalized trivia games. Anything romantic will do. We have presented a general list of things that most couples experience. Feel free to add your own special memories.

The song that was playing the first time you danced: _____

_____

_____

The first movie you saw together: _____

_____

_____

The place you first saw each other: _____

_____

_____

The song/fragrance/place that reminds you most of your lover: _____

_____

_____

The most romantic thing you ever did together: _____

_____

_____

Index